MANGO TREE TALES

MANGO TREE TALES

DEEPAK

PARTRIDGE

Copyright © 2016 by Deepak.

Cover Buddha Art Work By: Yogesh Phadke
Cover Design By: Santosham
Rishi Sketches and Review By: Anubhav Malik
Buddha and Rishi Sketches By : Anand Sapkale
KriSheo Publishing House

ISBN: Softcover   978-1-4828-6993-4
               eBook   978-1-4828-6992-7

Print information available on the last page.

To order additional copies of this book, contact
Partridge India
000 800 10062 62
orders.india@partridgepublishing.com

www.partridgepublishing.com/india

CONTENT MANGOES,

This Book is Dedicated to

BUDDHA

Acharya S N GOENKA

Bhavatu Sabba Mangalam
(May All beings be Happy)

Gratitude To Everyone

AAshirwaad (Blessings)

MyParents
Rishi Sheoraj / Mother Krishna

Chavi /Deepak

Neha / Poorvi / Tarun

Anubhav

Khushboo / Manuraj Teotia

AAshirwaad Rishis (Blessings From Rishis)

Bhogar Maharishi

Rishi Bhardwaja

Rishi Agastya

Rishi Panini

Saptarishi

AAshirwaad Rishis (Blessings From Rishis)

Mahavatar Babaji

Maharishi Amara

Rishi Tulsi Ram

Rishi Krishnananda

Swami Rama

Brahm Rishi
P V Vartak

Albert Einstein

Himalayas

Inspiration of Number 21

Dedicated To: Brahm Rishi P V Vartak Ji (website: www.drpvvartak.com)

And his article about travel to mars and Jupiter. After his astral travel to mars he gave 21 points about its environment. The number of stories i.e "21" is inspired from his 21 observations about mars environment.

Dr. P.V. Vartak is a renowned scholar who has been instrumental in unfolding many scientific facts from ancient Indian scriptures in Sanskrit and has presented it to the modern day generation in lucid and intelligible form. Besides being a spiritualist & a medical professional, he combines in himself the attributes of a Historian, Astronomer, Astrologer, Mathematician, Philosopher, Counsellor, Orator & Author.

He was born on 25 th Feb 1933 at Pune, Maharashtra, India. A seeker of truth, he does not differentiate between the followers of different religions and faiths & showers his spiritual love on the entire humanity indiscriminately.

Accessible even to a commoner, he has been giving spells of peace & solace to guidance and has been providing impeccable direction & succor even to a mundane seeker of help by rendering psychological & emotional support. He has kindled rightuous path for those who are in predicament over issues related to their profession, home or society. Foreigners are not exception to his transcendental love & blessings. He is an embodiment of spiritual realization and those in spiritual pursuits can take lessons from his personal conduct to have a better insight into what they just read in scriptures and find difficult to follow & assimilate. Having attained an exalted spiritual state, one can be more successful & useful even in worldly affairs and can prove to be an asset to the nation, rather entire humanity.

A distinguished rank holder throughout his academic career, he stood first in the London Chamber of Commerce Examination though papers were examined at London. A versatile genius, Dr.P.V. Vartak had been a 'body beautiful' champion, wrestler, swimmer and artist during his young age. He acted in dramas and authored one drama, rather an opera, namely 'Damayanti Parityaga'.

In his medical profession, he worked successfully as a lecturer in Surgery & Hon. Surgeon. In private practice he worked as Surgeon, Physician, Radiologist and Pathologist with highest medical ethics. He received Fellowship of United Writers' Association of India, (FUWAI) Chennai. The International University of contemporary studies has conferred upon him Doctorate of Philosophy in literature.

Married in 1961, he has two sons and a daughter. He commenced studies in Yoga and Spiritual Science in 1956 with highly analytical & scientific approach. Extra sensory perceptions have been experienced by him since 1959.

BOOK TITLE IS Inspired From Our InHouse Mango Tree
Tree Name -- RAMU

Four Birds

This is my story and "I" have named it "Four Birds" and who am "I" and what is my name you will come to know later in the story. So, Stay Tuned!

"It all started when Taani completed her 12th class exam and took admission in R.G College into Bachelor of Arts. It was her first day to college and her father gave her a 10 Rupee note for daily expenditure. 10 rupees were just sufficient to commute from her home to college and vice-versa. Her father had given her another 100 Rupees for emergency and instructed to use the money wisely. "Do not overspend. Do not eat road side food, it is not good for health" were his clear instructions to Taani.

He asked "Have you taken the lunch box"? Yes: Taani replied.

Taani left home for college. She walked down till the roadside local autorickshaw[1] stand besides a neem tree. People use to wait under the tree for the autorickshaw and hence it got the name as "Tree Stand". There were no signs of an official stand. As she was reaching the stand, she was feeling a beginning of a new life, a new chapter of college life. Her ways of commuting also were graduating from school cycle to college autorickshaw. While her mind was occupied with thoughts of new beginning, the autorickshaw's were same as before. She noticed an empty autorickshaw passed by her, she shouted "Wait, Wait" in not so loud voice waving her hand towards it. This was the first time she called for it. Autorickshaw stopped just ahead of the "Tree stand". It was a shared autorickshaw with a sitting capacity of about 6-8 people and she stepped inside and occupied one of the back seats. She was wearing white kurta salwar (traditional Indian dress for girls/women's which is very common in the cities of Northern India) with a combination of white dupatta. As she boarded the autorickshaw, she saw three other girls sitting there in the same dress code on the seat facing her. They exchanged a light glance (eye contact) and Taani promptly asked them "Are you going to R.G college"? They said yes. She introduced herself as Taani and said hello to them. Then they exchanged words of introduction about their names and

---

[1] **Autorickshaw** are a common means of public transportation in many countries in the world. An autorickshaw is a usually three-wheeled cabin cycle for private use and as a vehicle for hire.

departments amongst themselves. Taani appeared to be a shy girl but she has a habit of talking to the point.

First one to say hello was Pihu, girl who took admission in Bachelor of Commerce and then other introduced as "I am Era in Bachelor of Arts" and the last one said "I am Moni in Bachelor of commerce". They began to exchange more words about their family as auto rickshaw speeded up. Auto rickshaw stopped just before Begum Bridge. Begum Bridge was an important junction of roads. It was basically an important city centre crossing (meeting point of 5 roads) with different shops and different types of markets. One of the adjoining roads was famous for electronic products and the other one was famous for garment and hosiery market and the other had bus stand and sweet shops on it. And the one that goes to college had medical stores and several book stores shops on it. This was the way they need to take further. Auto rickshaw charged Rs 3 per person. The college was about more than a kilometer from Begum Bridge. From auto rickshaw stand they took a manual tricycle rickshaw till the college (all four of them) which charged them Rs 12, so Rs 3/person.

College was little inside from the main road. They left the rickshaw at college road and walked up till the college gate. So the one way expenditure till college was Rs 6/person.

As they entered the college gate they went to their respective department classrooms with some help. They attended the first day introduction session and got to know their colleagues in their respective classes. It was a usual introduction session.

During the interval they went to canteen and again met at the lunch table. Taani was a clear sighted girl. She used to always convey her mind well. She was not at all much talkative girl, but could communicate well with others. Pihu liked accounting very much. She was a little tom boyish and always flowing with ideas. Era was good at asking questions and was never hesitant in asking, if she could not understand the context. Moni was a bubbly girl by nature but used to follow others. They ate the lunch together in canteen and then departed to their respective classes. Taani asked Pihu to meet at the college gate in the evening. Era and Moni also said yes and they met at the college gate after their classes were over. Here Pihu said that she needs to call somebody urgently from PCO[2] (Public Call office) booth which

---

[2]   A **public call office** (**PCO**) is a telephone facility located in a public place in India and Pakistan. It is also another name in the United Kingdom for a public telephone box.

is about midway between college gate and autorickshaw stand. Pihu convinced Taani and others to walk down to autorickshaw stand. All of them agreed and started to move on the pathway alongside the main road. The road was usually crowded with traffic especially during the evening college end timings. Pihu moved up to the PCO booth and occupied the glass cabin with a single phone. All others stopped outside and waited while Pihu was busy calling up somebody. Taani was always curious about her surroundings and watched her laughing and giggling inside the sound proof glass cabin. She did not inquire about the same.

After Pihu finished her call, all four of them slowly started walking towards the autorickshaw stand. As they walked down the road they saw several vegetable hawkers. They could see fresh vegetables on road side shops and smelled different juices as there were many Juice corner shops offering a variety ranging from mango shakes to pomegranate, sweet lime, carrot and other juices along the way. Pihu and Taani were little behind Era and Moni who left a minute early while pihu was busy paying the change at the PCO booth. As they moved further they smelled a little sour and little different chow mein smell. Pihu turned to her left and saw a small road side hawker selling chow mein (a stir-fried chinese noodle dish) named "Cho Cho Chow mein". Taani also smelled and could not resist the smell. She got tempted to eat it. But she remembered her father's words to avoid road side food. By the time she could say anything Pihu was already there on the shop. She wanted to eat the chow mein and asked Taani to come over. Pihu could not resist roadside food, she was a complete road side foodie. By the time she tried to call Era and Moni they had already reached nearby auto stand. But before she could call them Taani said sorry I won't be able to eat with you. Pihu insisted but Taani refused. Though Taani felt the smell very enticing but refused. Pihu said ok, but I will eat and I cannot resist. Taani waited there while Pihu finished the chow mein. Era and Moni reached the stand and waited for Taani and Pihu. Taani and Pihu also joined after sometime and they boarded the rickshaw back home. Auto Rickshaw charged Rs 3 each same as in the morning ride. Taani asked the autorickshaw to stop first and unboarded near "Tree Stand" which is nearby her home. Rest of them stayed and left the rickshaw about 60 meters ahead of "Tree Stand" and walked to their respective homes. They all lived in a nearby residential society.

Taani's father asked Taani "How was the day"? She said ok and went to her room. Day passed and Taani again got ready to college with Rs 10 handed over by her father. Last day she saved Rupees 1 from Rs 10 as her total round trip expenditure was Rs 9. Taani's father asked her if Rs 10 was enough for the daily expenditure. He wanted to make sure whether it is enough or has she faced any problem in daily expenditures. So he asked once again, "Was it ok for the day"? She replied "It was ok dad".

Next day again she boarded the autorickshaw from Tree stand. Others also came over walking till the stand. They all boarded the same rickshaw and went to the college. They attended the college and in the evening they again decided to walk down along roadside till the autorickshaw stand at begum bridge. Pihu again stopped for calling from the PCO booth and same thing happened as they passed through the same "Cho Cho Chow mein" hawker. Smell attracted both Taani and Pihu. Pihu's road side foodie avtaar took over and she went up to the shop and asked Taani to join in. Today she also called in Era and Moni. Taani resisted again though she found the aroma quite pulling. She had never tried chow mein before. Pihu insisted again and then Taani said that his father had asked not to eat road side food. Pihu said but the quality is good, you can atleast try a little and then decide. Taani said that I do not have extra money for this. At this Pihu said do not worry I will pay and she called in Era and Moni also to share with her. Taani said that she will try but at one condition. Pihu said "What is that?" She said we all will contribute to it, as it is not good to eat daily on your behalf. If you are ok for this then I will join in. Pihu said done and they all joined hands together and Pihu named this pact as "1857 Pact".

At this, Era asked why the name "1857 Pact"?

Pihu replied "Ohh darling you are in Meerut". It is from here that India's First war for Independence began on 10th May 1857. It was a mutiny of sepoys of the East India Company's army from the cantonment area.

Era said "sorry, my general knowledge is little weak".

At this Pihu said this is called general awareness about the place you live in and not general knowledge.

Era smiled at her in a little embarrassed way.

Pihu paid Rs 20 for the chow mein. At which Era and Moni also said that it's tempting and good but they also cannot afford this daily. Moni said that she likes Samosa's (a common evening snacks in India) and Tea very much. Taani gave a smile towards her as if she agrees to her. Everyone really liked the chow mein and wanted to fall in this local road side food addiction. Taani told Pihu that she gets Rs 10 daily for the expenses and yesterday as they did not take the manual rickshaw from college to auto rickshaw stand she saved Rs 1. Same was the case with Era and Moni.

On this Pihu said I have a plan, ok let's do something. Let us save Rs 1 daily and by the end of the week i.e. after 5 days we would have Rs 20 i.e. cost of the chow mein plate. Moni said "I am in", Era said "I am also in" and finally they looked towards Taani, she also gave her signature smile. So, everyone agreed. But one plate was enough for only 2 or 3 people. Pihu said if required I will take on my own. That week they shared a plate and this is how gang started to form. So, once a week they use to enjoy that roadside chow mein and they felt like saving that 1 rupee daily. They all enjoyed the walk till the autorickshaw stand while coming back from college in the evening. This is where they use to mingle, chat, laugh, eat and shared their views.

They regularly attended the classes that week. Next week, Taani needed to buy some new books for her curriculum. So she came with Era and went to book shop nearby college. Pihu and Moni got a little late that day. As Taani went to book store, it started raining heavily outside. It was a sudden downpour and they did not even had an umbrella. She came to know from the shopkeeper that there is a bus stop just outside the shop and bus stops here for a short time and takes the route via Cantonment Railway station which was nearby their home. They could even take a small walk down home after that. As it was raining continuously, Taani and Era boarded the bus from that bus stop. Bus conductor asked them Rs4, Rs 2 each. Meanwhile as it was a weekend so Pihu and Moni stayed at the Cho Cho Chow mein and waited there for Taani and Era. But as it started raining they immediately moved to autorickshaw stand and boarded the seat back to home. Meanwhile Taani and Era left the bus at railway station. This was local cantonment railway station. It was basically an extension of the main city railway station and was used mainly by army people for luggage loading/unloading. So it was never crowded compared to main city railway station. Nearby the bus stop at railway station there was a tea and snacks stall named "Shiv Krupa" (meaning: Blessings of Lord Shiva). Taani knew about this shop as her younger brother sometimes used to bring samosas (a local north Indian snack) from this shop. It was a famous shop in that area. Taani and Era moved towards the shop. Rain also had stopped in the meanwhile and this was the first time "I" was introduced in the story. They asked Ramu kaka (old man who runs the tea stall) for tea/samosa price at which Ramu kaka said, see the rate board hanging just alongside the stall metallic door. It was written Rs 2 for Tea and Rs 3 for samosa. They both had Rs 10 as weeks saving, so they ordered 2 teas and 2 samosas. They enjoyed it as a rainy day treat.

After taking tea and samosa they looked towards me but I was little wet after rain, so they eat nearby the shop. This was my first encounter with two of them.

While they were eating the snacks, they saw Ramu kaka frying the famous bhaji (fried onion/potato mix north Indian snack). A bubbling sound of oil was erupting while Ramu kaka was flipping the bhaji in the frying pan. Once it is fried he took it out in a steel plate. It was ready to serve. It had a mild onion smell to it when served fresh. It had a crispy crunchy flavor at the top. When eaten the potatoes gave a soft feel to it with spicy flavor. Taani and Era observed bhaji frying in the pan and were tempted to eat it as well. But they stuck to their savings which was already finished and now they have to wait for next weekend.

After finishing the snacks they walked down towards home.

Next week, On Monday morning while going to college Taani and Era told Pihu about Friday's experience.

Pihu immediately said it's good and that she will also join in. At this Taani told that bus ticket charged them Rs 2 per person. On this, Pihu immediately said that we can try this option daily as it could save them 1 Rs extra. So instead of saving Rs 1 daily we can now save Rs 2/person and as the railway station is nearby so we can come home walking from station. At this Moni said what about your PCO date. Pihu smiled at her and said generally there is a PCO outside station as well. We will check this in the evening. They all agreed to try this as Taani also told about the samosa and tea they had at Shiv Krupa tea stall. After hearing about Samosa, Moni said "I am in", she will also come along.

After finishing the college they walked till the book store and boarded the bus to cantonment railway station. Since this was not the bus to main city railway station it was a little less crowded. Immediately they heard bus conductor saying that cantonment railway station is next, concerned people be ready to unboard. All four of them reached nearby front door and as bus stopped they left the bus there. Immediately they went nearby Shiv Krupa tea stall and looked towards "me" again. It was around 4 pm in the evening; the day was bright and clear (no rains). They started to come near "me" and as nobody else was sitting so they all sat on me. Yes, "I" was a bench outside cantonment station colored dark red with metal stripes at the back and base. Immediately, Moni said lets have tea and samosa's. Pihu and Moni went up to the shop. At this Taani and Era both said we won't have it you guys have it. At this Pihu said Ramu Kaka gives us four pegs of tea and four samosa. On hearing this Ramu Kaka asked what does "Tea peg" means, at which Pihu clarifies that means "four tea". "Ohh Ok"- kaka said.

While ordering, Moni saw kaka was also frying onion and potato bhaji. Moni smelled it. It was a mild onion smell which tempted her to taste it.

Though she knew deep fried stuff was not very healthy but still she could not resist and ordered one plate bhaji along with samosas and they chatted for a while sitting and relaxing over "me". Pihu and Moni paid for that day. And then Pihu said wait, I need to call some body. She went to the PCO booth which she has spotted even before looking at tea stall. It was towards left side of the station gate. Other three chatted for a while.

And from that day onwards, they used to come once a while on weekends to enjoy a sip of tea and samosas and crisp bhaji. They talked freely here enjoying the evening and use to walk down their homes together. I really enjoyed their stay and I used to listen to all their stories and experiences. It was a kind of unspoken/unseen bond between us. Since this was a small station (an extension to main one) so many other peoples used to relax sitting over "me". Frankly speaking I used to wait and long for their company on weekend evenings. I never got a chance to say hello vocally but I used to greet them always with my heart. This lasted for about three years during their college tenure. I use to wait for every weekend but many a weekends they used to skip may be spending their time at some other place. He didn't know they had another affair with temptation at "cho cho chow mein".

And it was that evening of June that they were enjoying their tea pegs, samosas and Bhaji, when Pihu said I have something to share, I am getting married after few months. Of course they had some idea as they had many a times waited for her PCO booth call to complete. But I was feeling sad that whether I would meet her again or not. But I never thought or imagined that it was their last evening with me.

And then they really never came there and I waited for them eagerly, daily, each weekend longing for their company. Now I just used to stare at birds in the sky and used to remember my "Four Birds"

Eight years later my memories were faded a bit so as my red color and I remembered them as my first love affair and just as "I" was about to sleep after evening late hours, "I" saw them again coming towards me. I was all charged up and refreshed. All my old meeting memories just passed my mind as they have happened yesterday only.

I was getting a little nervous and my heart was pounding little fast and then I heard Pihu saying in her signature tone, Ramu Kaka make us four pegs of tea and four samosas. On hearing four pegs of tea, Ramu kaka waited a bit and it took a while before he recalled them from his memory especially Pihu and asked them where were they all these years and asked about their well-being.

They started to chirp again and shared their experiences. Pihu lived in Meerut itself and was married to Shashank, same person she used to call quite often from PCO booth. Shashank is a business man and owns a restaurant chain in the city which was a hit some years back and is not doing that well these days. Taani said she has just moved in here and in meantime got married to a software engineer living in other city. She had come to take care of her in laws; who lives in Meerut itself. They had a daughter together. Era also got married and moved in here recently. Moni was silent and Taani asked about her well-being. She was just silent and did not even spoke a word. Later Taani came to know that she got divorced and now lives alone and works in a restaurant as a chief executive. They departed that evening and now occasionally come there to enjoy their time together. Moni was most of the time a silent listener. She was not like this when she was in college. Then one day while they were enjoying tea pegs, Pihu said friends I have a plan. I wanted to open a small restaurant of my own. Let us open it together. Era said I am in. Taani gave her signature smile and said I can also manage. Era then asked what would be the name. Pihu said "Cho cho Chow mein". At this Taani said I have a better idea. Let us use first letter's of our names in title name. Pihu said suggest something. Taani said "T", "P", "E", "M" and it started here at station, so let it be,

"TEMP" + "TATION"= "TEMPTATION".

Pihu and Era said brilliant, let's do it. Then they started a restaurant named "TEMPTATION" as it came out of their affair with temptation and their resistance of temptation. It reminded them of their good old days. They named the dishes as:

1: "Cho Cho Chow mein"
2: 1 Tea peg with sugar/ without sugar
3: Crispy Bhaji
4: Mr. Sam (i.e Samosa)

It all started well and they made the arrangements and put the benches inside instead of chairs (could be attributed to "me", atleast "I" would like to believe that) along with tables where benches resemble their station bench where they spent their good old days.

It also made Moni little occupied and relaxed. She started to see her life in a new light. Slowly and gradually she also became lively and regained her old charm back.

Good old friend groups use to gather here and use to remember their olds days. This was a hit from day one. It became an instant hit with youth groups and old age groups. People from all ages started to visit and enjoy their get togetherness.

This worked well for them and then one evening after a year they saw a gang of four girls sitting there and ordering "Cho Cho Chow mein" and Tea Pegs. Pihu immediately got nostalgic and looked towards Moni, She said I am In, Era also looked towards Moni and nodded in eyes and then looked towards Taani who smiled and they immediately left for railway station. Instead of car they took the Bus and reached the station in their old style.

At station as they approached "me", they said amongst themselves that "Nest" has an old bird in it. Yes "Nest" was the name they had given me. Yes there was an old lady sitting at one side of the bench having tea and samosa. May be she also could not resist her temptation for tea and samosa. We all are same they said to each other.

They also sat on "me" and ordered four tea pegs and samosa's.

Suddenly Pihu said I have an idea, Moni said "I am in" even before listening.

Era said what's the idea? Pihu said lets open a club. Era said "name". On this Taani said the same "Temptation" and after having tea and samosa they moved away walking towards their home…

This was my story and I remember all the good bad and lonely days but surely it was the affair of my life…It still is…

With Love → From "Nest"

Be Happy
Bhavatu Sabba Mangalam

PEELU – THE YELLOW FRIEND

———◆———

It's a Saturday 6:30 am in the morning and Krishnkant is dusting his bicycle for the day's ride. He has just finished oiling it. He does it on the weekends. On weekdays he attends the University Botany department. He works as an assistant professor at the city university in botany department. He is a plant lover and is passionate about his work. He had always wanted to work in botany field. Years ago he applied in the department as a botany research assistant. He got the government job and based on his research work he is now promoted to an assistant professor's post. He is now known as a botany specialist and is a scientist by nature. He loves to explore the flora and fauna of various areas in and around his place.

He lives in Pune city in a multi-story building on 4th floor. He lives there with his son Chetan and his wife. Chetan his son is 10 year old boy. He is attending a regular school.

His passion to explore the flora fauna makes him visit the nearby Malshej Ghat[3] each weekend. Pune is a hilly area and comes under western ghat belt. Pune is surrounded by many ghats on all sides. One such ghat is Malshej ghat. It is very rich in flora and fauna.

He comes upstairs after cleaning the bicycle and reads the local news column in the daily newspaper. He reads a caption and gets very enthusiastic and calls his wife that "look there is an article about a new species of frog found in malshej ghat". He gets even more excited after reading the article. Malshej ghat has become a hub of new research in flora and fauna area. Many people are working independently exploring the area. As his weekend passion, he is also preparing to explore there today.

He waters his basil plant in the balcony before leaving for Malshej Ghat on his bicycle. He waters it every day. Chetan also observes this daily and as a habit he has also started to water the plant. They had kept the basil plant pot in the balcony area. It is considered auspicious to have a basil plant in house. Chetan often asks his father about the benefits of keeping the basil plant. Krishnkant had told him about the medicinal properties of the basil plant.

———

[3] **Malshej Ghat** is a mountain pass in the Western Ghats range in the Pune district of Maharashtra, India.

He tells him that basil leaves can be used in tea or can directly be chewed. It is very helpful in cold and some other ailments. Chetan is also turning into a plant lover inspired from the passion his father has for them.

Krishnkant is now leaving for the ghat. Today chetan also insists on going with him. Krishnkant tells him that it's a little far. It is about 15 km from here and you have to sit on the front side of bicycle. "It will be a little tiring for you", he tells Chetan. These were his immediate suggestions to Chetan. If he listens to his heart then could easily see that he wanted to take Chetan along as he could see his developing interest in plants. He has noticed in Chetan taking good care of his plants. He is aware of the fact that such small trips can sometimes acts as a very good trigger for propelling future interest. But somewhere at the back of his mind he knew that it's a little risky trip in that area due to its hilly terrain. He wanted to avoid that. But Chetan still insists to come along. Krishnkant finally says "ok", you can come along but on one condition; you will not go any side too far on your own. You will have to be with me all the time. Chetan agrees to this condition and commits that he will be around him always. On this Krishnkant agrees and Chetan puts on his shoes for the day and takes his cap on his father's suggestion. Mother had prepared the tiffin (with some extra snacks for Chetan) for the afternoon lunch and asks krishnkant to take good care of Chetan. Mother also instructs Chetan separately to not lose sight of his father. They both leave for the ghat.

They reached the site in time and father parks the cycle and moves towards exploring his current interested area. He continued at the same area where he visited last time for exploration.

It is a plateau area with some steep curves along with adjacent valleys around it. He takes Chetan along and starts exploring that area. He opens his cotton bag and takes the camera out. He puts that around his neck. He has a little polythene bag to collect the latest samples.

Krishnkant's current area of interest is to explore new fungi species in that area. He has been working on this for quite some time now. He had previously found one new species for which he was recognized at the state level. It is his ambition to make it to the world level scientific community. He has faced some hurdles publishing his new research in past.

Krishnkant immerse deeper in exploring the new plant and fungi species in that area. Chetan also started to explore the surroundings. While his father gets more involved collecting the samples and taking the photos of the fungis, Chetan also roamed around a bit asking questions about the surroundings to his father. He was always near him till now. Meanwhile Krishnkant get engrossed and could not take note of Chetan. This time Chetan went a little away from him and found a big rock nearby. He just went on the other side of the rock. There he found a bunch of dense trees as if something is behind them. He was about to go further, as he heard his father's voice "Chetan where are you?" Chetan replied "coming father". Krishnkant tells him not to visit that side. Next time please make a note of this. Chetan agreed to this politely by nodding his head in affirmation. They explored some more and took the lunch in the afternoon. Chetan asked his father about the research process and sample collection. His father explains him in detail about the sample collection and its analysis. Chetan listens to his father with a sharp focus. By then Krishnkant got some basic samples and thought of returning back in the evening time. They both wore their sun caps and reverted back to home.

He has to check the samples for any probable matches. He thought of doing it in the coming week. First he needs to prepare the culture report. Any new samples need to be matched. This process will take some time. But somehow he had a feeling that it might already be present in the global database. Still he will proceed with the work.

Chetan also gets busy in his studies. In the meanwhile something strange happened with Chetan, he started to get some dreams. He was able to recall these dreams in the morning. He narrates about this to his mother. He tells her that he saw an entity talking to him and wants to be friends with him. Mother was busy in preparing the breakfast and said "Do not worry. It was just a dream". Dreams sometimes are a little weird. Do not bother and get ready for the school.

Chetan gets ready and leaves for the school. Chetan was good at studies and has a hobby of drawing sketches. He was good at it too. He got a very good grade on previous weeks sketch home work. Class Teacher distributed last week's sketched papers with the grading. Chetan returns home and shows that to his mother. Mother was delighted to see the progress.

Meanwhile, Krishnkant got busy in his regular botany lectures. Alongside he is also doing his sampling work for the collected samples. He has made some significant progress this time.

Chetan again gets the same dream about the entity and he again narrates it to his mother. Mother becomes curious and asks him to explain in detail. He said there is one entity who wants to be friends with him. Entity said his name is "Peelu". On hearing this mother said nice dream and please get ready for school.

On the coming weekend Krishnkant again plans to visit Malshej ghat area. This saturday they both again went to Malshej ghat. This time Chetan tries to remain along with his father all the time. His father gets busy in his regular exploration work. Chetan takes a break for some time and goes away for toilet and immediately ran towards the other side of the big rock which has dense bushes behind it. He went close by those dense bushes. And as he approached a little closer he could see a little cave covered with some bushes. It seems nobody ever came this way. This was a kind of a dead end. As he went a little closer he could exactly see a cave. He was excited to enter it. He cleared the bushes with his hands and as he entered the cave he was amazed at the sight. Just then he heard his father call. He was shouting, "Chetan, Where are you"? Chetan said "coming father". Chetan wanted to stay there but ran to his father's call. Immediately a bunch of monkey's jumped from above the bushes. Chetan got frightened and ran toward the valley. In a sense of hurry, he slipped his feet and fell down into valley. It was a deep valley. There was no chance of his getting alive. Father had heard his call but when Chetan did not come for long time, he went there. He could not find him and as he looked below the valley he saw Chetan's dead body over a big rock in the base of the valley. He started crying and could not believe his eyes as Chetan was with him sometimes back. He wept there for hours in this shock and returned home late. Looking at Krishnkant's swollen eyes; mother asked "Where is our son?" Father cried like anything and narrated her about the incident. Mother fell apart on hearing this. For some time she didn't knew how to react. She also started weeping there along with Krishnkant. She said, "I told you to take care of Chetan". It's your fault, she cries again. This was shock to both of them as if their little world has fallen apart.

Krishnkant along with few neighbors goes to the police station and tells about this incident to police officer. Police goes to the place where incident happened and recovers Chetan's body from the valley. This incident was a turning point in their lives and everything changed after this.

Krishnkant lost all his interest in any further research. He took a long leave and hardly takes any lecture these days. His wife is very much worried about him. He never visited that place again. His wife is taking care of Krishnkant and prays to god for his well being. After a month, Krishnkant seems to again regain his lost interest and starts to visit the college for his normal lecture work. She feels relieved to some extent.

Few more months passed and as he fits into the normal college routine and just when their life starts to again come back to normalcy, he started to see some strange dreams in the morning hours. He saw some entity in the dream. He ignored it for some time. One fine day he got the dream very prominently and he just wakes up in hurry. His wife was at bedside and got worried about his husband. She then asked him about the dream. She gave him a glass of water. They both sat down on dining table and he narrated the dream to her. She then recalled about the incident where Chetan once told him about the similar dream. She kept quiet and asked Krishnkant to forget about it. She feared that her husband might again fell in depression state and it would be really hard to pull him again. But she thought about Chetan's dream incident when she was alone. She did not know what to do.

One day she was sitting at the dining table after Krishnkant had left for the college. She decided to clean the house as a daily work. As she was cleaning the drawer she found out Chetan's sketches and got emotional after looking at that. She takes a break and sits on the chair and started to think about Chetan. Her eyes are wet again and she sleeps there on chair itself. Once she gets up and looks at the sketch again, she is amazed to see that Chetan's school sketch contains an entity named "peelu" – yellow colored entity on one side and Chetan standing on the other side. She could not make out anything from this drawing. But she remembered Chetan once told her about the entity. She decides to talk about this to Krishnkant when he will come back from the college today. She also remembers about similar dream which Krishnkant is getting these days.

Krishnkant returns from the college in the evening and rings the house bell. She comes to open the door. Krishnkant freshens up and she serves the evening tea. Krishnkant sees the sketch lying on the table and puts the cup on the table. He immediately says it's the same entity he is seeing in his dreams these days. She comes and sits at the table and tells Krishnkant that Chetan also once told her about the similar dream. She ignored it at that time but today she found his sketch having the details of the entity. They both discussed the matter for some time and mutually decide that there could be some message behind this sketch. They should dig a little deeper into this matter. As a plan of action, Krishnkant decides to visit that place again where the accident happened. But his wife is little frightened as it is the same place where Chetan got slipped. It reminded her of the old memories about her son.

She asked Krishnkant not to visit the place.

Krishnkant replied, "Do not worry, I will take care of myself".

She said that she will also come along then, at which Krishnkant insisted that he has a good idea of that rocky terrain. Do not worry; he will take care of himself. He asked her to stay back.

Krishnkant once again dusts his cycle in the morning and leaves for the ghat. She hands over the tiffin and asked him to take care of himself and be cautious. Krishkant was little sad but wanted to pursue this matter. He went to malshej ghat and after parking his cycle he walks to that big rock spot with dense bushes. After looking for some time behind the big rock, he saw there was a dense bush and he felt as if some cavity is behind this bush. He cleared the bushes with his hands and saw that there is a cave behind that. As he cleared more he could see a light emitting from the floor. He went inside to have a closer look. He was astonished what he saw next. The whole floor was covered with yellow light emitting fungi. He has never seen anything like this before in his whole life. He could not believe his eyes for some time. He has never seen or read about light emitting fungi. It's a rare species he thinks. He picks up some samples and collects it in his sample polythene bag. He now thinks about the dream which he is getting since last many days. It is this entity who wants to get discovered first through Chetan and now through himself. He looks towards the sky and remembers Chetan. He takes a picture of the fungi. After returning home he shows the samples to his wife. She also gets excited to see this amazing species and remembers Chetan who wanted to narrate his dream to her. Next day he reports this to the college authorities and they went there to have a look. Krishnkant gets a nod from the college head to pursue this one. Department head asks Krishnkant to prepare and submit the reports to the international journal "Nature" as soon as possible. Krishnkant was a little excited to pursue the work. He was feeling a new vigor and energy in his exploration journey. He felt really grateful to god for giving him such a nice opportunity. He really was fully revived after the current set of events.

After few weeks he submits his initial report in a journal and after some days gets a notification about the new species. He names it "Peelu" (The word Chetan use to utter when he use to narrate his dream).

Krishnkant and his wife both decide to make a small stone memorial point named "Peelu – in fond memory of their son Chetan".

His father becomes a renowned botanist with this discovery.

He is now retired and still remembers his son a lot. In his fond memory he visits that spot once a while.

His father forms a group of likeminded botanists and zoologist and now spends his time promoting the research in that area. He now has one more area to explore and that is "How plant communicates through dreams/visions". He finds this really interesting to pursue.

Be Happy
Bhavatu Sabba Mangalam

LOVE IN HIROSHIMA: WORLD WAR 2

"Little Boy" was dropped at 8:15 AM on August 6, 1945. He can feel the burning sun at his cheeks on this hot cloudless morning. He looked up the sky and saw the beautiful silver airplane with white long tail and the blue sky. It looked beautiful receding farther away from him each second. He looked as if it was his last look. He is cruising down towards the earth below piercing the wind and is about 2000 feet above the ground just over the target, the famous T Bridge. Fate still has some seconds in hand.

Few days back, life was moving smoothly in Hiroshima, Japan completely unaware of what is going on in American camps. As usual life had no stop, it picked up pace as the day dawned in city of Hiroshima. It was yet another day in Hiroshima's calendar. The day was bright and sunny. The day was 3rd August, 1945.

Akio and Akira both were childhood friends and shared a very close bond. Their parents were also close friends so many say that they also got their friendship in heredity. They shared each and everything and were like two bodies with one soul. Akio was a little extrovert and Akira was a little introvert but wiser of the two. He could see the things in their true sense. But he never took advantage of it.

Akira usually would keep his feelings with himself but would give genuine advice to Akio in face of adversity. Akira was a little shy of showing them externally.

They had similar choices in life and both tend to tilt towards the same option. This was little unusual but it was true.

And it happened once more when this morning they both saw Kiyomi. Kiyomi was a beauty from who's magic nobody could escape. They both were mesmerized by Kiyomi's beauty. Kiyomi was talk of the town. Many other tried to chase her but nobody could grab even her attention. They both looked at Kiyomi and it was love at first sight for both of them. Kiyomi saw them in awe and just passed by smilingly. This seems to be positive sign and they both were feeling first love breeze. Each of them is unaware of the other's feeling. Whole night they could not sleep. Both started to dream of Kiyomi until next day when they saw her again near T bridge.

Akio asked Akira isn't she beautiful?

Akira said who?

Akio said "Kiyomi who else".

Akira was just thinking of sharing his feelings with Akio as he also fell for the same girl. Before he could confess his love for kiyomi to Akio. Akio said she is my dream girl. I will marry her one day. Till this time Akira was unaware of Akio's extreme feeling towards Kiyomi. But after Akio's confession he decided to remain silent and kept his feelings hidden in his heart only.

Seeing no response from Akira's side Akio asked "What's the matter"?

Akira said "nothing".

Akio said tell me why are you so silent? "Is everything ok"?

Akira gave a blank look towards Akio which he was unable to grasp.

Akio could not even guess the smell of feelings germinating in Akira heart towards kiyomi. Akio was so awestruck by kiyomi's beauty that he was just thinking about himself and could not even notice that they both were in the same boat.

Akio asked Akira to help him to propose Kiyomi. He is not sure how he should go about it. He needs a wiser advice and who else can he look up to apart from his childhood friend, his dear friend Akira who had always helped him in such times.

Kiyomi was all over in their dreams. They could not think of anything else. They had seen kiyomi just once and they both fell in love with her. They didn't even know where she lives.

Akira due to some reason was avoiding the discussion at this time. Akio sensed this and decided to go as per his plans. He could not wait anymore and bought a ring for her. He was planning to propose kiyomi near the famous T Bridge. The day was 6th Aug, 1945. He showed the ring to Akira. Akira gave a casual nod to him by which Akio was unable to make out whether he liked it or not. He somehow was sensing that Akira has grown cold towards this matter and is not giving his honest advice. He could not sense why. He was just thinking of that sweet smile she gave while passing by them. He was just bowled over by that smile.

Akira asked Akio "you have seen her just once and not even met her don't you think it is too early to propose"?

Akio replied that he really loves her and he couldn't wait anymore.

Akira had no reaction this time. Thinking realistically, Akira could see that Akio and Kiyomi's relationship might not work.

At this, Akira said let's do it as we always do. Akio says, ok then take the coin out. Toss the coin let's see what god has to say.

Akira said if it's Tails then you will propose today, if it's Heads then not. He still not had shown his feelings towards kiyomi. Akio was still unaware of it.

Akio said ok and says that I know god is with me this time. I will win the toss and her heart too. Akira tossed the coin and Akio saw that it was Heads. He was heartbroken. He still did not want to go by this result. He felt hearts matter cannot be decided by a mere toss.

By this time "Little Boy" reached at about 1900 feet above the famous T Bridge when suddenly they saw an explosion. The first bomb was dropped on Hiroshima. It was a sudden attack. Within a flash of a second, it spread 3 miles over the city and mushroom cloud could be seen spreading as high as 10 miles above the city. It converted downtown Hiroshima to a wasteland. It exploded about 45 seconds after it was dropped from the airplane. The streets that were filled with people are now filled with carbon debris. Some people even vaporized and others turned to carbon with in a fraction of a second. It was really a horrific sight. Amidst these both Akio and Akira also ran for their life and managed to enter in the nearby underground dungeon.

Akio and Akira could not think what has happened. They both could not believe the sight. They just hid in one of the corners of an underground dungeon. Despite of such a disaster outside, Akio still could not get over with kiyomi's thought. Akira said, I think we will be safe here.

After about an hour as they felt little hungry and started to move to other corner. Akio was amazed to see Kiyomi in front of him. She was also hiding their perhaps. His heart started to pound profusely just at the sight of kiyomi. He could not believe his eyes at first. Akira also came there and saw kiyomi in front.

Just after few seconds Akira noticed that Kiyomi was advancing towards Akio. Akio felt glad and did not know how to react. Seeing Kiyomi advancing like this Akira jumped in between them.

Akira shouted "Run away Akio.. Run away Akio.. Run fast..".

Akio could not understand what he is saying. Till the time he could understand and do anything Kiyomi galloped Akira in front of his eyes and ran away. Akio now came to his senses and shouted Akira - no, no Akira you cannot leave me.

Akira was still shouting "Run away Akio, Run for your life" while fighting his last battle in Kiyomi's mouth. Akio cried and cried but could not save Akira. He wept like anything for hours.

Akira had fallen prey to deadly Lizard kiyomi. Lizard loves cockroaches especially when it's hunger call.

After hours he managed to pull himself up and walked slowly towards one corner. While moving back Akio saw the coin in that corner. He picked that up as his friend's last memory. As he turned the coin he saw heads. He flipped it again and saw heads at the other side also. He cried and deep gratitude arose in his heart. "Akira my friend you saved my life, God Bless You", he blessed him from the bottom of his heart. He sat there at that corner remembering Akira his true friend. Drops of black rain could be seen in the city as if somebody is crying from above.

"Little Boy's" body is cremated or vaporized which even he did not know but his soul is surely alive and could see the landscape covered with unending carbon debris. Black rain is emitting from the depths of his heart. The devastation is tremendous which anybody could hardly imagine in his dreams. Some people vaporized in this tremendous heat and others turned to carbon ashes immediately. Little boy could see them from above and at the same time felt a deep sense of remorse and forgiveness for all the affected souls. In his deep feeling of forgiveness, the following lines just flowed effortlessly through his mouth:

> Little boy from sky above,
> Little boy from earth below,
> Little boy from near the bridge,
> Little boy was "sometimes" back,
> Little boy is no more body,
> Little boy is now a soul,
> Little boy was not alone,
> Little boy with other souls,
> Little boy had tears in eyes,
> Little boy with a heavy heart,
> Little Boy humbly said,
> Forgive me all, Forgive me all…

Inside the dungeon, Akio kept the coin for his life to come. He still lives in that dungeon after that nuclear attack. He has nowhere to go. He comes to that corner each month to remember Akira, his true friend. "May god bless you my friend" his hearts wishes for Akira. He never saw Kiyomi again.

May be she is in some other dungeon. As they truly say lizards and cockroaches can remain alive even in nuclear holocaust.

Be Happy
Bhavatu Sabba Mangalam

RAMU DIARIES: THE MANGO ART

———◆❖◆———

"Lakshmi, what are you staring at through the window. There's nobody out there dear. Please come inside it's been very long" says the mother to Lakshmi. Lakshmi is still standing there and looking towards their garden tree outside. She is still there despite of her mother calling several times. She does it quite often and stands at their prayer room window watching the tree sometimes for long hours. The garden tree is clearly visible from the window. She does respond in her baby tone which her mother only understands. She is just one and half year old and learning to speak as her vocal cords are still infants. She murmurs few words as a response in her peculiar baby language. But this time mother pulls her away and takes her to the other room where her father is getting ready for days work.

Guru has just taken a morning bath and is getting ready for the day's work. While breakfast is getting ready, Guru does his daily rituals before taking the food. He picks up the empty diya[4] and lits it up in his prayer room in front of the gods. Lakshmi sees this daily with a sense of curiosity and accompanies her father in this act. As a precautionary measure so that Lakshmi does not get burnt he always takes the diya and keeps that on the kitchen side unit's shelve. Guru takes the empty container, a water bottle and moves towards the back side garden gate. He also takes Lakshmi in his arm lap and opens the garden door. As he enters the garden balcony, he keeps the container and water bottle on the wall. He now fills container with water from the bottle. Lakshmi is still in his lap. He takes the container in one corner of the garden hedge and offers the water to the shivling[5] (Symbol of Shiva Deity) established there. It's a family Shivling and is kept over a brick base. He takes Lord Shiva's blessing three times and blesses Lakshmi also by putting his hand on her forehead. Then he

---

4   **Diya** is an oil lamp, usually made from clay, with a cotton wick dipped in ghee or vegetable oils. Clay diyas are often used temporarily as lighting for special occasions such as festival of diwali in india.

5   **Shivling** is a representation of the Hindu deity Shiva used for worship in temples. In traditional Indian society, the Sivling is rather seen as a symbol of the energy and potential of God, Shiva himself.

fills up the container again and offers water to the Sun deity and fills up the container again and moves towards the other end of garden. There are several basil plants scattered all over the garden. Some are small ones and others are fully grownups. One such fully grown plant was at far end of the garden. He offers the water to that basil plant and offers his good wishes and takes blessings of the plant. Lakshmi is part of these acts as her father accompanies her daily. While returning back guru daily stops in between near the mango tree. He along with Lakshmi greets the tree with a "Good Morning". It's a sort of morning hello to their in house neighbor. Lakshmi also feels the leaves and plays with them while still in her father's arm lap.

She is part of these daily morning rituals and it seems like she also has started forming a bond with the tree. She loves this part each morning and is really happy being near the tree. Guru also feels good for her as he himself is a plant lover and takes care of his plants well. He is also happy as he observes that Lakshmi is also imbibing some of these traits. These are childhood days and guru feels the seeds sown now are very important all through a child's life. He is a nature lover and has a firm belief in nature's laws. He himself believes that life is like a tree, as you sow so shall you reap. The type of tree depends on the type of seeds you have sown and used to follow same practice which he has inherited from his parents.

Guru comes inside from the garden door and sees that breakfast is ready on the dining table. He eats the breakfast and leaves for work. Lakshmi is also getting ready to take the morning bath. Mother takes her to bath room.

Guru returns home little late in the evening and chats with his wife at the dining table. He tells his wife that they recorded a song today. He is a co-producer in a feature film for a production house and they have just finished some pre-production work. Song came up nicely and guru is really happy for the same.

He is also starting his own family business and is working towards that. He has a vision of setting up his own movie production company. He started the work with his colleagues for the same. But he has a feeling that work is not progressing that well. He wants to finish up the company logo first. They have started with logo design sometimes back. They outsourced the logo design work to one design firm. Initial work was promising and he reviewed it for finalization. But he always felt that something was missing and it never clicked. He had given few trials and was not fully satisfied with the company's prototype designs. The logo work was stalled for some time due to this block. Today also he had one such meeting for the logo finalization. He is still not satisfied. He has started thinking of hiring another company for the logo design. He is feeling that something is missing. He feels that first thing should be done first and it should be a good start. He feels that logo is the first step, once it gets finalized everything else will follow. He retires to his bedroom with this thought occupying his mind.

Next morning as usual he takes Lakshmi along for the morning rituals and leaves for the work. His work was occasional. Some days used to be busy while others are comparatively free.

Next day he has off (no work) and asks his colleagues to come over his home for the logo finalization discussion.

He is hoping to have some productive meeting and will decide on hiring new design firm based on the outcome of this meeting. He reviewed the design and the same jinx continued. As he was coming downstairs he was little frustrated as work was somehow coming to a halt. As he reached the last staircase he saw Lakshmi showing her hands towards him. She wanted him to take her in his lap. Guru was a little frustrated and casually scolded the child. She started to cry.

She went to the prayer room window and wept there for some time and then stayed there staring at tree. It was little unusual but by now her parents knew she used to stare mango tree for long hours as if she is having a silent communication. Mother consoles the child. Mother had observed this behavior and use to take her away from window many a times. Mother did not like this attitude of Guru towards Lakshmi. She feels that work should not interfere with child's upbringing.

Guru departed for an urgent production work and returned a little late that night. He was getting busy in his current film production work. They were thinking of improvising the recorded song for their movie. The first version needed some improvisations. That day they had a long meeting with the music director. He came late and directly went to his bedroom.

Next morning as usual he accompanied Lakshmi for the daily rituals. While they stopped by Mango tree, Lakshmi started to point her fingers towards a bunch of leaves. She also said something in her infant voice which Guru was unable to understand. He saw towards those leaves but could not locate anything. Lakshmi continued to point towards those leaves.

He could not make out why she is pointing towards those leaves.

Guru came inside and left for the work that day.

Next day again when they stopped at mango tree, she started to point her fingers towards a bunch of leaves as if she is looking at something. He thought perhaps she is pointing towards mangoes. Tree is now filled with this season's mango crop. He could see dozens of them but they had not plucked a single mango this season. He comes inside and asks his wife to take note of the fallen mangoes. He asked her if she happens to find any fallen mango on the ground then they should be offered to gods first and it should not be eaten. He asked her to keep that in their prayer room. First one should be offered to Lord Krishna.

That day when Guru returned from the work at night he went directly to prayer room. He many a times meditates at night before going to bed. That day he also found Lakshmi standing there by the window. He sensed as if a silent conversation is going on between the two, Lakshmi and the tree. He knew that Lakshmi sometimes stands by the window staring the tree. But this was the first time he saw her in night. He got a little worried and asked his wife to take Lakshmi to the other room. He also departs to his room after the session.

Next day again the same thing happened and as he took Lakshmi near the tree she pointed her hands in that one direction. He could not figure out why. Then he thought of checking a bit more towards the lower branches. He saw that there is small shell hung from a thread on one of the lower branches. He remembered that he had himself hung that there. He thought Lakshmi is pointing towards that. He has a hobby of collecting stones and shells from the beach area. But he still could not figure out why.

They came in again and he shared this incident with his wife. She said that why you are so worried about that. She is a child must be pointing towards some mango or something. She took it in a casual manner.

Again the next day while returning back after watering the basil plant he stopped to say "Good Morning" to the mango tree as usual. Again Lakshmi started to point her hand towards those leaves. This time he thought let's explore it little closely and as he went close by he found that there is green mango just behind the leaves. As he observed it closely he saw that there is a little design with some white marks on that mango. He thought perhaps she was pointing towards that. It was little unusual design but it caught his attention immediately. He went inside and brought his camera. He took a snap of that mango. Since it was a little windy that day, he got a blur snap.

He left for the work that day but that design got stuck in his mind. He shared this information with his graphic design team. Design team immediately agreed to check that out. Guru could see the faint design and could resemble it a little bit. But he asked his design team to make it clearer. He shared the image with them.

Design team member applied some image processing functions to get a clear image. After processing they saw that it was a swastika sign on that mango. Design person shared the improvised image with Guru and tells guru that it's a swastika sign and tells him it is very auspicious. Guru knew about the auspiciousness of the swastika sign. Guru immediately asked them that "Can you include this swastika sign in our old logo design to get a new hybrid design". They said we will work on the logo again and will try to incorporate it. Guru waited eagerly for their first version.

Guru was not very sure how they could fuse it in the current logo design. But the graphic artist called him in the evening to review the design when free. Guru reviewed it the next day. He had fused the swastika design at the back of the logo and it was looking much nicer. It immediately clicked with Guru and he thought it is perfect.

He showed that one to his wife and she also agreed for the same.

Next day he plucked that mango and offered it to Lord Krishna. He kept that in their prayer room.

His business started to grow, he had some fruitful meetings after that. He was now happy with the way things were shaping. He thought of it as a gift from his daughter and blessed her from his heart. He was still astonished and could not believe that something as subtle as design could be inspired from a mango art. Messages can come from anywhere. Nature works in mysterious ways. His faith in nature started to take even more firm ground after this incident.

He is now a successful entrepreneur and keeps that mango art snap in his office. He framed it and it is now on one of the office walls.

Lakshmi still goes to that window and engages in a silent conversation with that mango tree. It's a telepathic communication between the two.

Guru sees this and is relieved that there is another plant lover in the house. Seeds are sown and he wishes this to continue and thanks nature for the same.

Few years later..

Lakshmi has now learnt to speak and she speaks clearly now.

She still stands by and stares the mango tree as if in silent communication. Now she also says the name "RAMU" once in a while. This is the name they have given to their mango tree. They had also put a name plate with name "RAMU" just beside the tree. Now everybody in their neighborhood calls him by his name. He still serves the family with lots of mangoes each season.

Regular Morning: Guru says to Lakshmi, I am going to meet Ramu.. Lakshmi says wait daddy, I will join you in a second.…

Be Happy
Bhavatu Sabba Mangalam

CHRISTMAS BELL

It was a sunny winter morning in Pune and I was just coming in from my backyard garden balcony gate when I happened to see the dilapidated condition of my BSA mach one cycle. I now have my own bungalow flat. The cycle was kept lying adjacent to the side wall in the open tiled floored space besides the garden. The cycle body was covered with lot of dust and rust. The cycle was my close companion in my bachelorhood days when I use to wander on it to different places. Some times in night; sometimes in broad daylight she accompanied me like a devotee. Sometimes I used to talk and sometimes whisper in her ears. She was an apt listener and has always taken care of me. At that glance I felt like I am neglecting her now and a strong feeling of injustice towards her current state came to me. I now feel that the entities (in this case my cycle) also has a consciousness and they are livings beings in itself. Any piece of machinery which helps us in some work has a consciousness of its own. It gave me a chance of retrospection in my own psyche. And I came to a conclusion that it has become my habit in general, to neglect my things. That moment in time was the moment of realization and revelation at the same time. A very strong feeling of gratitude arose towards her and it reminded me of my Christmas Bell wish fulfillment story.

"It started in 1997 winters in Agra. I still remember the 24th December mid night. It was dark and cold with ample amount of fog in air, visibility was low but anybody could see ahead clearly for about 50 meters. Just through the room window, I could see the halogen lamp on the outside electric pole verifying the visibility limits. Beside that window, I was sitting on my chair engaging myself in the preparations for the forthcoming engineering exams. I had a wooden table with lots of books piled up neatly on one side of it and a small study lamp with a 60 watt bulb on the other side. Just a few meters ahead in right side corner was a small spider web with spider resting in the middle of web. As usual, I used to feed him the banana in small bites. I used to throw these small bites towards the web. With 2-3 bites sticking inside, I wanted to observe their eating habits. Banana and spiders were a weird combination but I still wanted to try this one. I saw he walked smoothly on the web towards the banana pieces and stick to it for some time. After few second's spider left the banana bite and moved again at the corner of web.

This was a little local research experiment with spiders and also a means of refreshment in between study breaks. As I was just over with this experiment and was thinking about my physics problem, suddenly I heard a loud sound of church bells. I was immediately attracted to this sound of bells. There was a church nearby that place which I have never visited even once. That was the first temptation of visiting the church. On hearing the sound of church bells a desire arose within me to be in that atmosphere of church, experience every bit of happenings in church on that day. The thought of being there on 25th December celebration just moved me. Immediately after hearing the bell I ran out of my room. There was a small covered verandah which had a wooden metal sheet frame to partition it from outside open verandah. I opened the verandah door to step in the outside verandah and went towards the door. At one corner of the outside verandah there was a small wooden door. I opened the door and started to look in the direction from where the bell sound was coming. I could not see the church from there but could feel the vibration of the bell. The temptation of the sound bell pulled me towards it.

It was strange and very exciting feeling but somehow I could not step out in search of church that night. But the memory of bell sound stayed within me in my sub-conscious and I thought if someday I will get the opportunity then I will definitely go there. I did not know that time how it will culminate. I continued with my preparations.

Year later I got into JEE and moved to ISM Dhanbad for my engineering studies. After completing the engineering I moved to Pune in 2004, where I started my life as a Software executive.

Here in Pune I met Naveen a fellow colleague at my I.T. company Infonox Software Pvt. Ltd. He was working in company's in house call center. He used to live in Paraplegic centre near Khadki which was about 3-4 km from Baner, the company's office. It was year 2005 and I was normally working at my desk when George my fellow colleague uttered that Christmas is nearby. But this time it is Sunday (so one leave has lapsed). It got my attention then and there. I thought that we are just a week behind from Christmas. The Christmas bell started to ring in my ears enticing me to celebrate this year's Christmas at any one of the church, not sure which one. I had seen just one church in Pune that was nearby Paraplegic centre in Khadki. I have seen this one on my visit's to Naveen's place. I decided to visit that church on coming Christmas night. It was Saturday on 24th December and I was there at my rented apartment. As the evening was approaching I was getting excited to visit the church. It was a long wait. I left my apartment room in Baner on my cycle at the night time around 9-10 pm after taking some dinner. I paddled to khadki via Parihaar

Chowk on my cycle alone. I used to enjoy such alone trips at that time. They were meditative for me. It was just me and my cycle. The cranky sound of cycle chain use to add an extra flavor to those dates with alone night rides. Mostly, I used to go to Naveen's residence at Paraplegic centre. I always noticed the big banyan tree on the right side with its long signature branch offshoots running from top towards mother earth. The empty bus stop at night used to remind me of the variations life offers busy in the day and stillness in the night. Stillness, silence has always attracted me to fathom more into them. Seers say that the answers to all the questions can be found in silence. It appears to me an interesting path to follow. A glimpse of that I used to feel in these alone night rides.

As I paddled more, I passed the Monginis cake shop towards the left and saw a sign board stating that "Khadki railway station" is straight and "Khadki cantonment Board" is towards right. Right was turn I need to take. It was dark and as I was approaching the right turn I saw a scooter passed by me with a very high speed. I noticed a Santa Claus sitting on the scooter's back seat. Perhaps he was also rushing towards the church. I sailed towards Paraplegic rehabilitation centre and reached at Naveen's place at around 11 pm. Church was nearby from this place so I thought of parking my cycle at his place. I was unaware of any parking at the church premises. I parked my cycle in front of his room in the long corridor. There were several adjacent rooms in a row. It was for armed forces only. We chatted for some time and then I left the centre on foot walking slowly towards the church. I reached at St Thomas church gate after a while. The semi circular gate was lit with lightings made of small bulbs all over the gate periphery. On the way towards entry there were some beggars sitting on both side of the entry way. Many of them were women with children's in their lap. This was little unusual site at the gate but is a reality of the society. Positive side of it gives people the opportunity of gaining merits of alms donation.

I walked inside the main gate towards the main church building door. As I walked alongside the church building I could see the beautiful lighting all over the building. The semicircular lighting in different colors was just adding glitters to whole of the building top from outside. It was looking magnificent. I took a small right turn to reach the main entrance door. As I reached at the door; the view was magnanimous with ornate golden color statue of cross visible exactly at the far end of the room amidst the group of big white candles fixed at their stands. The golden color decoration was adding a royal touch to the sacred cross. I could also see the Jesus Christ mural painting at the top of the back wall with white angels on both the sides.

A large group of people have gathered for the Christmas mass prayer. They were also waiting for the prayer procession to start. After a while people started to chant the prayer in hall. For some time I could not understand the language. Then as the mass prayer progressed, I got to know that it is not in English. I did not know this before and thought it to be an English church. But despite of that I started to enjoy the prayer. The cumulative energy of the chorus was at a different level. My every ooze was feeling it. I attended the full prayer despite of being a different language. The prayer hall has a pathway at the centre acting as a partition for men sitting to the left and all the women and children's sitting to the right side of it. There, midway in that path was a small wooden charity box. The church was beautifully decorated from inside. The "Father" was standing just in front of the cross statute with the same Santa Claus who passed by me on scooter, standing beside him. Just above the "father" there was a decoration piece hanging from the roof with a cotton Santa Claus draped in traditional red color with a bell and two rein deer's on both sides. On the top of it was written "Merry Christmas". I saw that and wished everyone in the church "Merry Christmas" from my heart. Father had a big white beard wearing a black gown with yellow collar stripes with a black cap at the top of his head.

It went on till about 1 AM in morning. I felt happy that finally I attended one Christmas celebration after so many years. At the end of it everybody moved ahead in a queue along that middle path. I also followed everyone and slowly progressed. As the queue approached near the front of the hall we saw that each person was getting one big piece of cake. A Christmas feast it was for me. I also got one. I could now see clearly the golden color cross statue with all its intricate designs. The Jesus Christ painting at the top with two angels on both sides was clearly visible from here. I bowed to him in gratitude. As I raised my head again I received a piece of cake. It was a small nice experience receiving that Christmas cake at the end of it. The experience was worth it and then everyone moved out from the left door leading outside the hall in the corridor. Everyone walked down the corridor reaching again towards the front of hall door. It was a small circular journey resembling the circle of life in some way. I stayed there at the front hall door for some time as if assimilating my whole experience. Then I saw that there was a small camp fire arrangement at the front. People stayed and sang carols moving and dancing around the fire. It was yet another treat to be a part of this ceremony. I stayed there and enjoyed every bit of it. Just when I was about to leave, I felt a hand on my right shoulder from the back side. I turned back and was surprised to see George there. He was my colleague at the company and I was least expecting him at that church. We greeted each other "Merry Christmas" and shared our Christmas night experiences. During the discussion he told me that this is a Malyalam (an Indian regional language) church. The language mystery was finally solved at the end. We both ate our piece of cake together and said good bye to each other. I bid farewell to that church one last time and walked out towards paraplegic centre to pick up my cycle. The experience was unique and precious one for me. It was my first experience in any church on a Christmas night. I thanked again to the "Church" for a memorable night.

As it was already late in the night so I decided not to disturb anybody at the centre and unlocked my cycle and started my small journey back towards my rented Baner apartment. It was around 2 AM then and it still was a long way back. I paddled all through the lonely route alone at night. I still remember the sound of chain coming to my ears in deafness of that black night. This is how that "Christmas Bell" was finally culminated. Though I did not hear the real bell at that church but still while travelling back this thought came to my mind that Christmas Bell has finally rang for me after so many years. That desire of mine was fulfilled. Though I was alone cycling back home at night time but still I felt really happy at the core of my heart. This is how my "Christmas Bell" which started in cold Agra night rang finally in Pune. I was relieved and happy".

After this story passed through my mind's canvas I was still standing besides my cycle. I thought of cleaning it and did the same and draped its body and wheels with newspaper and polythene. As I moved away I heard a voice saying "Thank You for Taking Care". I immediately turned towards cycle as if she was talking to me. I stood there for some time looking at it and Thanked back for teaching me the value of care.

It is fully functional again and I now use it for my casual work like shopping etc. She is back again.

Be Happy
Bhavatu Sabba Mangalam

KHABRI AND SHABRI: TEA TIME

---※◆◈◆※---

Today is festival of Diwali (an ancient Hindu festival which signifies the victory of light over darkness) and Shabri is busy preparing some traditional meals at home for dinner. She loves to cook traditional food whenever she gets an opportunity. On diwali night Hindus dress up in new clothes, light up lamp and candles at each corner of their home. After preparing the dinner she also lighted up diyas and candles. She is very fond of fancy diyas[6] and she buys one big fancy diya each year. This diya looked beautiful when placed at the centre of the drawing room just over a colorful rangoli[7] which she finished up at the day time. She is still busy now and does necessary preparations for Lakshmi (Goddess of wealth) Puja[8]. Lakshmi puja is one of the important rituals performed during the festival of Diwali. This ritual is performed to invite Goddess Lakshmi at home. Prayers are offered to the Goddess so that the New Year (Hindu New Year) is filled with peace, wealth and prosperity. Everybody enjoys the dinner after puja is over and gets ready to celebrate diwali with a community fireworks show. Most of the family inmates of their locality gather outside at a common verandah each year. This is more like an evening diwali get together for all of them. Each family brings their own firecrackers and turn by turn they lit up all. The firecracker show is always a hit amongst children's. Amongst the light in darkness, amongst the sound of crackers, amongst the sweets of festival, the dark moonless night became even more young and cheerful than the bright afternoon. Greeting for each other came effortlessly from the heart and everyone exchanged the packet of words named "Happy Diwali" filled with light and happiness. The get together got over a little after fireworks are finished. She also returned to her apartment and directly goes to her room. She remembers that tomorrow is Govardhan

---

[6] **Diya** is an oil lamp, usually made from clay, with a cotton wick dipped in ghee or vegetable oils. Clay diyas are often used temporarily as lighting for special occasions such as festival of diwali in india.

[7] **Rangoli** is a folk art from India in which patterns are created on the floor in living rooms or courtyards using materials such as colored sand or flower petals etc.

[8] **Pūjā** is a prayer ritual performed by Hindus to host, honor and worship one or more deities, or to spiritually celebrate an event.

puja. She is aware that it will require some early preparations. She thinks that, "she will consult her mother in the morning". For that she will have to wake up early. Shabri has already taken office leave for tomorrow.

She wakes up early and gets ready for the Govardhan puja (this puja generally is performed on the next day of Diwali laxmi puja) preparations. She is more than willing to assist her mother in all puja preparations. There is a tradition of building cow dung hillocks, which symbolize with Mount Govardhan, the mountain which was once lifted by Lord Krishna. After making such hillocks people decorate them with flowers and then worship them. They move in a circle; round the cow dung hillocks and offer prayers to Lord Govardhan. Each year her mother also builds their in-house Govardhan cow dung hillock at their backyard garden floor. This year due to some urgency the cow dung was not available. Though her mother had asked their maid to bring in some cow dung for the puja but she could not arrange it. Plan B became active and her mother thought of an alternative for building the Govardhan hillock. It was when their family use to live in Mathura area that her mother learned to prepare the Govardhan hillock with wheat flour and turmeric powder. She did exactly the same this time. This was something new for Shabri and she found her mother quick in managing things. An idea came to her mind that, "Why not make a video recording for the same". She also executed that in minutes. "This will be a nice memory for future reference", she thinks. Each year after the puja her mother prepares the recipe for Annakut which also she learned when they use to live in Mathura area. This curry is first offered to the deity then later it is distributed to all in the form of prasad[9]. This is the recipe dedicated to Mother Annapurna (Hindu goddess of food and nourishment) and is prepared from different vegetables mixed together. It is a very simple recipe in ingredients and very nourishing. She got curious and this is the first time she has asked her mother about the basic recipe preparation for Annakut. Mother likes this and asks to accompany her in the preparations. Before that; mother asks her to take something for the cold. She finds that Shabri is suffering from cold these days. She gives her ginger paste mixed with fresh honey. "Take it, it's good for cold", she says. Shabri hugs her mother. Mother has already started the preparations. She immediately agrees to assist her mother for the same. Her mother notices that, "Shabri is actively taking interest in their household traditions this year. She

---

[9] **Prasad** (also called **prasada** or **prasadam**) is a material substance of food that is a religious offering in both Hinduism and Sikhism.

finds it as a good sign for her growth". Shabri is smart and meanwhile she again thinks of capturing a home video of this preparation. This will help her later and will be a nice video learning tutorial. While she was busy shooting the video she got a message from Khabri about the next day's plan. Shabri reads the message and smiles as if she has something in mind. Next two days are the weekend days. Shabri finishes the video and notes down the recipe ingredients in her golden book. She has one golden book where she writes all her favorite recipes. She has a streak for recipe innovation and has some new recipes in her book. She likes to innovate whenever she gets a chance. She always gets interested whenever she comes across a new recipe idea. She has developed this new taste of recipe innovation and exploration just over the last year. This golden book is basically a diary for keeping records. It has become her habit to write all the new recipes in her Golden book.

Khabri is currently working in an I.T Company as a software lead but is basically a poet at heart. He has acquired the skill of poetry just over the last year. He was imaginative before also but the imagination embroidered with reality is taking him in the deeper realms of the poetic world. Whenever Shabri sends a message to him he always replies in the form of an original piece of poetry. This has become his subconscious pattern now. He is least interested in mobile phone messaging. For him his mobile phone is a device just for making and receiving important calls. As a result his store of forwarded message is almost nil. But he still likes to keep his poetic replies in his sent folder. He has not deleted even a single one and looks at them once a while for creative inspiration. He always thinks that he should reply the message with something original and he does so each and every time. As shabri has a little cold these days about which khabri is aware of. He advises her to take ginger and basil tea. Though Khabri is least interested in the messages but somehow he never ignores Sahbri's message. He sometimes even waits for her message. Slowly and steadily he is getting inside the world of messaging. Shabri is working as Human Resource(HR) executive in one of the HR firms. She has done her Master's in Business Administration with specialization in Human Resources. She has joined the company recently and is getting good opportunity to learn the work.

Their first meeting was purely by chance. Shabri met Khabri for the first time at a tea stall outside her company premises. Khabri's IT Company was also in the same compound as Shabri's. Khabri happens to see Shabri for the first time at a tea stall just outside the compound. She had a cold that day and came out for a casual tea. It was a common tea stall in the whole compound and employees from different companies use to come there for a casual break. Khabri also used to prefer the same tea stall. By chance, Shabri kept her company employee card at the tea stall corner table and Khabri also kept his at the same place. Khabri was about to pick it up just then he got a phone call from his manager who wanted him to come urgently. Meanwhile Shabri asked the tea stall owner to put some ginger powder in her tea. Tea stall owner puts some in her tea only as he always prepares the tea for all in one go. After finishing the tea she picks up the card and returned to her company. While Shabri tried to swipe the card at her company entrance she realised that it is not working. When she looked at the card closely she found it of some person named Khabri. Same happened with Khabri wherein he also realized that card is not working. They had no other option but come again at the stall. They both came back at the tea stall looking for one another and met again. This is how they met consciously for the first time while exchanging their cards. Something strike with both of them and after that first meeting, tea stall became their occasional meeting point.

Khabri has no personal vehicle as of now and mainly commutes by foot between his rented apartment and company. All his friends have their own motorbikes and some even come to office by car. He never competes with them and this area has never bothered him. He likes enjoying a walk to his apartment. While travelling in the city he takes either a lift or hires a private vehicle. He lives in a rented apartment near his company premises. Apart from the tea stall sometimes occasionally they use to meet at the evening time after office hours. These meetings were also by chance. Khabri never initiated this move by himself. He was a pedestrian and whenever Shabri happens to see him walking besides the road she use to stop by and offer him lift till his apartment. Khabri use to always refuse the lifts. Though they meet occasionally at tea stall but still khabri had never taken lift from her. Shabri sometimes could not read his mind but was attracted to Khabri's simplicity and honest behavior from that first meeting. She knew that Khabri would prefer walking then to take lift as Khabri's apartment was nearby his company premises. This was Shabri's take on his behavior.

And then it happened one day. Once khabri had to meet his friend in town and as usual he was walking by road side when Shabri saw him walking very fast. She came near and stopped her scooter besides him. She offered him the lift as usual. Khabri also halted and after looking at both the sides he agreed for the lift. He was trying to hire private vehicle but could not find any. Shabri noted this day in her mind. This is the first time he has agreed for the lift. She asked him about the drop point. Khabri replied and asked her to stop at the city university circle. Shabri finds this as a good opportunity for a nice discussion. They had various discussions while driving towards the University circle. She discussed his poetry while driving. By now Shabri has become fond of his poetic replies and finds them sometimes unique, sometimes inspirational, sometimes touching the romantic chord. Now Khabri once a while started to take Shabri's lift while going to meet his friend. They use to discuss about poetry, city forts and many other things. Sometimes she uses to feel as if Khabri is saying something from back. But when she used to turn her face back as if asking him "What is it?" she use to notice khabri is quietly sitting at the back seat. Even khabri use to find this strange sometimes. Nobody knew what it was but surely there was some exchange between them, may be a telepathic connection. During those lonely rides Shabri found out about his love for old Shivaji[10] forts in and around the city.

Shabri had sent a message to khabri about the weekend trip last night. Before leaving the house this morning she completed her morning Gopal Ji (Child avatar of Lord Krishna) puja. She use to daily bathe him in the milk and change his clothes before lighting up the diya(lamp). She told her mother in a hurry that she will be going on a trip to Singhad fort with a friend. Mother inquired, "Which friend" but by then she had already left the lobby. Shabri took her scooter out from the porch and started it. She gave a little throttle to accelerator and went outside very fast. Shabri was taking keen interest in khabri and she has started to like him more with each meeting. She also had sent one message on khabri's mobile phone this morning. Khabri reads the message and thinks about it. By now, khabri has already reached at their meeting point near city circle lamp post. He is waiting for Shabri since last couple of minutes to pick him up. It was a weekend day and they have planned a trip to Singhad fort nearby the city. Khabri has fascination and interest in old Shivaji forts. One of them is the Singhad fort about 30 km from city of Pune. As he was moving back and forth at the lamp post, he saw her from a distance. He stood there waiting for her. Shabri reached there after a while and khabri smiled looking at her. She also gave back a sweet smile. Khabri took the back seat and they went ahead for the fort.

Singhad Fort is at a higher sea level than the city area. It is a plateau area at the top of hill. The curvy road has an upward slope with a repairing work going on for some portion in between. As they were reaching near the fort they passed many turns on upward road. One such turn has an old Ganesha

---

[10] **Shivaji** also known as **Chhatrapati Shivaji Maharaj**, was an Indian warrior king and a member of the Bhonsle Maratha clan.

statute under a corner tree. The road there was a little uneven and rough due to the ongoing repair work. They took a small break there and again further continued towards the top. This was their first trip together to Singhad fort. As they reached the top plateau, she parked the scooter in parking. They could see a narrow staircase route going up till the fort entry gate. The route was carved out in rocks with long staircase steps. It has a dark reddish texture and had several local food hawkers sitting mainly on one side of the route. One such hawker was selling raw mango pieces with a little salt and pepper spread over it. Shabri could not resist and bought some. It tasted a little sour but was a nice companion upside the big rocky uneven stairs.

They moved slowly discussing about the message.

Shabri: So what do you think about the plan?
Khabri: Which plan?
Shabri: The morning message. Did you check that?
Khabri: Yes of course. I liked the idea. I never thought we could come up with such a nice plan.
Shabri: Then where is my first one.
Khabri: Wait for the moment.
Shabri: Ohh.. so you also have a plan..
Khabri: Hmm…

They walked upside the steep staircases leading to the fort entry gate. There are several hawkers sitting at both sides of the staircase. Once this is passed they can move around on the leveled slope. They walked upside the concrete pathways inside the fort area. It is a fort but it does not have a ceiling. It only has a rocky boundary that too uneven and missing at several places. There is cave towards the left side just after the entry gate. Some of the visitors went inside but Khabri and Shabri both went ahead.

As they move ahead they could see group of hawkers at both sides of the pathway. These hawkers are basically villagers mainly village women's from in and around Pune. They usually have small huts made of husk, bricks and wooden logs for preparing the local food. They have small trees outside these huts acting as small canopies underneath which the visitors can sit over the plastic carpet to enjoy their meals. They serve one special meal called "Juna Bhakar".The meal comprises of the bread(Indian roti) made of Jowar, meshed bringal dish (baigan bharta) and gram flour kadi along with some butter milk which is optional. The meal is really tasty and takes the taste buds to another level. This meal is very popular amongst the local people. Apart from this meal they also sell kanda bhaji (crispy snacks made of onions and gram flour) which when served with hot tea will act as a nice evening snacks. Visitors love this one especially in the rainy season. For meals you have to sit on the ground over a plastic carpet. It feels very satisfying sitting under a tree and having a nice meal breathing a hill top fresh and energetic air. It is really a rejuvenating experience.

As Khabri and Shabri walked over the pathway they also heard these hawkers. Instead of stopping at one of them, they first went straight to the last fort gate which is at the far end of fort and also a little below the main fort plateau area. It is a little tricky route reaching there but the view is really breath taking. The black stone gate has steep and uneven stairs down the hill. They spent some quiet time there at the stairs. There were about 30 steps going down till the last point. Reaching till there crossing those uneven rocky steps was a treat in itself. The view of a vast open valley after that will mesmerize anyone. The steps were a little uneven so both of them took care while moving down the stairs. Shabri was a little reluctant in the start but when khabri insisted, she also took it as a challenge. It finally paid off as the view from there was awesome. This was first time Shabri had come this far at the fort. Khabri knew every corner of it. At one side they could see some remains of the old fort walls. They sat there for some time enjoying the view and started a casual conversation.

Shabri: Why do you come to office by foot?

Khabri: I feel like exploring the things from basic. First step first and then second.

Though I can afford a two wheeler but still I wanted to start on the foot and then will move on to buying a two wheeler and so on... Let's see how my journey will shape up..

Shabri: You are a little strange in this approach. If you can afford some luxury then why don't you take that? It seems like you have some vision of your own.

Khabri: I have always followed my heart and will continue to do so... I might be alone sometimes but this is my way.

Shabri: Hmm.. You always reply with a piece of poetry in return of my messages. Do you have a store?

Khabri: No, I do not have much forwarded messages. In fact I do not get any forwarded messages. I like doing original things. So before replying, I always thought what original I can do in this situation. I try to send you an original piece each time.

Shabri: It has worked till now.. She smiles… Where is my latest one?

Khabri: Give me a piece of paper and a pen.

Shabri: I do not have it right now.

Khabri: Ok. Let me write it on my mobile phone.

Shabri: Hmm.. Gave a soft look..

Khabri: A little ginger, A little basil,
A little sugar, some leaf of tea.
Milk Milk where are you,
Come here soon, Come here early,
We want to make a sweet top hill,
We want to make a hill top nice Shabri tea…
To Shabri – At Singhad Fort
Take it in cold… It's good for you… Smiley

Khabri: Message sent. Check now.

Shabri: Checking the message. I got your "Soft Tea". Really nice. She sends a smiley back. Where is your hard Tea.

Khabri: "Soft Tea"? I didn't get you.

Shabri: Yes you have just sent me a message Tea.. It is a Soft Tea. Now let us have a real one.

Khabri: Hmm.. Just wait, I will order now.
Khabri orders tea and some kanda bhaji from a hawker alongside.

Khabri: Clicks a hill top selfie and frame freezes…

Be Happy
Bhavatu Sabba Mangalam

THIRD EYE BOOK

Pali is looking at the visiting card and feeling as if something is missing on the back side of it. Visiting or Business cards have the person's details and designation along with the company's name on the front side. Usually the business cards are empty at the back side. But she was feeling a strange kind of void at the back side of it. It was constantly appealing to her that there should be something at the back side of card either in Sanskrit or in Hindi. She was thinking for some shlokas[11] or some inspirational phrase but could not decide for the same. She parked her thought on that for time being and indulged herself in other works. She got involved in over-looking their online start-up business. She was thinking of their online website work for which they have hired a professional website development firm. She was monitoring the development work and continued with the change iterations on weekends. They were having regular meetings with the development firm regarding the changes.

Manu is a meditator turning into an entrepreneur who is starting his new carrier in creative field. He has dreams of making it big in publishing industry.

He has got some ideas for novels and stories. He wanted to develop them in his own style and is working for the same before getting launched into the market. Many of the ideas are in infant and seed stage. Some of them are already seeing the light of the day. He is into the process of establishing the new business but is waiting for the right time. Manu is very particular about his heart's call. His policy is wait and do. He waits for the right moment and the inner call for starting anything. This approach creates a little uneasiness amongst his close family members and friends but he likes to execute it this way. Sometimes the wait is too much and people around him feel uneasy and frustrated.

---

[11] **Shloka** (meaning "song", from the root *śru*, "hear") is a category of verse line developed from the Vedic Anustubh. It is the basis for Indian epic verse, and may be considered the Indian verse form *par excellence*, occurring, as it does, far more frequently than any other meter in classical Sanskrit poetry. The *Mahabharata* and *Ramayana*, for example, are written almost exclusively in shlokas.

He has attended a writing workshop along with his office job on one of the weekends. It was a batch of around ten people from different fields and different age groups ranging from youngster to company directors. It is at this workshop that they met each other for the first time. Some of the members are still in touch over the chat messaging groups and meet once in a while over a cup of coffee. One such group that got formed is of these three Manu, Chandra and Mihir.

He is constantly in touch with Chandra and Mihir, the other two people in the group. They all bonded over a short film script named "My Mom Is My Angel". They use to have regular meetings for discussing the story plot and developing the script which also included some deep discussion about the character profile. It is after many such meetings that they came up with the final draft of the script. Once the script was ready they started to discuss the direction and treatment details. They also included some songs and poems in the script. During these free thought meetings the mind used to flow and used to wander in different directions. It was a kind of bonding over a script work. Many new discussions were spawned form there. The work that was done there was a free flow hearts work. Everybody bonded well over the discussions.

That script never saw the light of the day but the bond continued and the youngest one, Mihir thought of starting his family business and online store. He wanted to make a one stop solution for different kind of services. He started his family business and invited the other two at his inaugural puja[12].

After the puja got over there was a photo session for all the members along with the company's logo in the laptop. The laptop had a company's logo as a desktop background image and everybody decided to have a round of photo sessions with the same. It is at this time that Manu saw a little Bhagavad Gita book lying there at the side corner of the table. Manu took the book and placed it in front of the laptop. Photos were taken afterwards and the book was present there in many such photos of the evening. After that the photos were copied back to the same laptop and everybody enjoyed the evening photos on it. The photos with the book were a little different but stayed there somewhere in Manu's subconscious mind. That day was also a festival of Raksha Bandhan[13] where Mihir's elder sister Pali tied the rakhi(sacred

---

[12] **Pūjā** is a prayer ritual performed by Hindus to host, honour and worship one or more deities, or to spiritually celebrate an event.

[13] On **Raksha Bandhan**, sisters tie a rakhi (sacred thread) on her brother's wrist. This symbolizes the sister's love and prayers for her brother's well-being, and the brother's lifelong vow to protect her.

thread) to all of us present there. It was a small inaugural event with close family members and us. His father conducted the puja and aarti[14] along with his mother. There was a traditional cap which belonged to his father and was gifted to him in his marriage from his wife's side. Everybody wore the cap before taking the rakhi ceremony snaps. The evening was nice and traditional. Everybody took the prasadam[15] at the end. The puja and rakhi ceremony was over and we all gathered in the puja room sitting down on the floor for an initial round of discussion about the company's functioning. Mihir offered some snacks to all of us. Manu got a call from his pregnant wife. She was worried as it really got late that night. Manu left for home after finishing up the discussion and reached quite late at home that day.

Next morning Manu could not sat for his regular meditation at his usual place but he moved to another bedroom where his pregnant wife was sleeping along with their daughter. He sat there for some time while they were still asleep. He immediately went into meditative state. Just after Manu started meditation the body became erect in lotus posture and energy began to rise through the spine. The head became erect as if fixed without even the slightest movement. The flow of electricity began to move up and down inside the body. The sitting continued for some time and after a while Manu started to feel as if a book is flapping / opening at his third eye. This session continued for about twenty minutes and then after a while he was able to feel it as the book of Bhagavad Gita. This process of opening of third eye book continued for some time and immediately after this Manu automatically started to recite "Bhavatu Sabba Mangalam" and it continued for another twenty minutes or so. Manu did not consciously recite this mantra but it came out all of a sudden continuously. While in this state Manu kept his right palm on his pregnant wife and recited "Bhavatu Sabba Mangalam" for quite some time. He did the same for his daughter who was sleeping alongside his wife. After this session, he got a concrete vision regarding some information. The information was

---

[14]   Aartis also refer to the songs sung in praise of the deity, when lamps are being offered.

[15]   **Prasad** (Hindustani pronunciation: [prəsaːd̪]; also called **prasada** or **prasadam**) is a material substance of food that is a religious offering in both Hinduism and Sikhism. It is normally consumed by worshippers. 'Prasad' literally means a gracious gift. It denotes anything, typically an edible food, that is first offered to a deity, saint, Perfect Master or an avatar, and then distributed in His or Her name to their followers or others as a good sign.

regarding Mihir's start up. He saw a completely different set of positions (aka designations) compared to what exists today.

After few days he met Mihir while driving towards the local market. He offered him lift and they both began to move towards the market. In the midway Manu hinted him regarding the channeled information about the start up, which he felt during Third eye meditation session. It was surely a message from higher planes. After a small discussion Manu came back to his home and dropped Mihir nearby his home. Few days later; Mihir and Pali came to Manu's house and they discussed the details about the vision.

The information was channeled in the form of continuous 10-15 minute session where Manu happened to walk through the positions (aka designation) one by one. He saw that the owner was seen along with a golden pot and the position that came for him was Chief Money Sevak[16]. He communicated the same to him. Also during the vision he saw that Pali was shown with the birds and the position that came for her was Chief Bird Sevak. Then he saw his father who was a scientist. He saw all the information in form of pictures. He saw his father along with a basil plant. The position that came for him was Chief Plant Sevak. Then came his mother, the position that came for her was a guardian angel. She will protect them all. Then other positions were channeled for the group. The position that came for Chandra was Chief Commitment Officer. The position that came for Manu was chief sevak. One information that came for Manu's wife was of Chief Bird commissioner. He communicated the same to his wife at which she laughed casually. This also prompted for a new kind of photo session for all of them where first Mihir would be shown along with a golden pot, his sister would be shown with a bird and his father would be shown with a plant. Same goes with their Visiting cards. Each of them will be shown as per their positions. Mihir will have a golden pot alongside his image on the card and same for all others as per their respective positions. Chief sevak will be seen along with other people's head. After this discussion was over everybody took a tea and now they shared some facts about the information which came as a counter validation for this channeled information.

Mihir told them that as per astrological readings his good time has already started. His sister told Manu that she used to love birds right form her childhood. And their father after getting retired gifted basil plants to his close friends. It was nice to hear about the confirmation about this channeled information.

---

[16] **Sevak**: One who serve others in the specific context.

Also some additional information got channeled. Manu told them about this as well. It was that every new deal should be named after a bird in the company's internal references. This could be an internal/in house document where every deal will be named after a bird and his sister should take care of that. Also every client should be gifted one Bhagavad Gita book when the deal is finalized, with a company visiting card inside it.

Till now everything is fine and then came the question from his sister Pali who was sitting alongside. She said that she was thinking of printing something at the back side of their visiting/business cards. She said that she has pondered over it many times but nothing strikes her convincingly. What should it be?

Manu said adding to the channeled information that he also saw one Sanskrit shloka at the back of company visiting card.

Pali: Ohh that's a very good coincidence, she became enthusiastic and
          asked in "What was the shloka"?

Manu said, that each visiting card should be printed with the following Bhagavad Gita shloka at the back of it.

Shloka in Sanskrit: *"Karmanye Vadhikaraste, Ma phaleshou kada chana,*
                Ma Karma Phala Hetur Bhurmatey Sangostva Akarmani"
Meaning: *Do your duty and be detached from its outcome, do not be driven by*
                the end product, enjoy the process of getting there.

It resonated with everybody and they were astonished to know that such things happen in real. They nodded with affirmation. Everyone was happy and relaxed. Manu handed over this piece of information on paper to them. This is how the Third Eye Book ended...

                                                Be Happy
                                                Bhavatu Sabba Mangalam

Paap Ka Ghada ya Maitri ka Ghada (Sinners Pot or Merit Pot)

Bhavesh has just reached office in the morning. He boards an office bus daily for commuting office. He has skipped his breakfast at office canteen today and directly heads to his cubicle. He seems a little anxious today and unlocks the computer at his desk in a hurry as if he is waiting for something.

He opens Microsoft outlook and checks the reply of his last mail. He saw one reply mail. His heart started to pound as if he is sensing something wrong. He opens the mail and finds that Global Business Head has responded positively considering his points and clarifications. She assured that she will look into the matter and suggested that he should also talk to his division head in Germany. He felt a little relieved that someone listens to the truth in the company. His faith is still on with this reply.

But the storm is still not over, infact it has just started for Bhavesh. These were the initial cyclonic winds. Much more is awaited further for which he needs to get prepared. He is feeling nervous but still he is not giving it up. He wants to bring the current situation to forefront which as per his opinion is causing much distress among the fellow workers, which in turn is affecting the work environment. As per his understanding this is also affecting the business prospects of his division in the company.

Most importantly, he is facing it himself which is acting as the main trigger. Some of his fellow colleagues are aware about this situation but nobody wants to point it out. There are some others who are ok with this as they are receiving favors from their seniors. He takes the baton and comes forwards in pointing out the situation. He has vomited his current state and all the points he faced during past month into his last mail; yesterday before leaving the office.

He has to vomit as he could not contain it inside anymore. He left little early yesterday after framing this mail and has kept in loop all the heads of his unit as well as some of the concerned heads of the company.

"It all started one year ago when Bhavesh gave interview for the position of Sales profile. His first interview round was telephonic and his final round

43

happened on skype[17]. Akash, manager of MCD division took his final round and shared the salary structure with him.

Akash asked him to review the salary structure; which Bhavesh did after the call and replied to Akash about some errors in the calculations and some other clarifications. At this Akash got little annoyed and called up Bhavesh on his personal mobile phone and said that you should have asked about these errors and clarifications during the call.

To this Bhavesh replied that he checked the salary structure only after the interview so how could he have done it during the call. Akash got annoyed even more and asked him that he will not tolerate this attitude. Even after all this Bhavesh got the offer letter and joined as a business executive.

Bhavesh after spending about 10 days in company guest house rented a shared apartment nearby his company premises in Pune. He was previously working in another city. He started working in late shift as assigned by Akash.

He has started to adjust himself in his routine work. He got engrossed in his day to day office work and three months have already passed by. Then one day his manager, Akash asked him to join in the noon shift (Europe timings) as one person has resigned from that shift and it needed an immediate attention. Bhavesh accepted the situation and started working in noon shift. His work capacity also became smooth as he was in the day time (which are natural working hours). He used to commute daily by walk as he was residing nearby his company office. He was giving good output and was balancing both work and his personal life. This rhythm was working well for him. Once in a while he had to work late which was fine with him. He continued in this shift for about six months now. He had no personal vehicle of his own and was thinking of buying one.

In the meantime, it was announced that company will be shifting to (HP park phase 3) new location. Now this location was a little far as compared to the current location. As per agreement with the house owner (landlord), he rented the house for about a year. So he will have to commute from this place only.

For all the employees in day shift; company started a bus service, which would leave office by 6 pm in the evening. But as Bhavesh timings (for Europe

---

[17] **Skype** is a telecommunications application software product that specializes in providing video chat and voice calls from computers, tablets and mobile devices via the Internet to other devices or telephones/smartphones.

shift) were till 8pm; he would have to most probably rely on his own vehicle which he did not have as yet.

He started working in the day shifts in new location and for few days he commuted by bus service. He informed Akash that he would be leaving a little early by 6 PM evening bus for few days. This arrangement worked for couple of days, but as work pressure grew more he had to work till 8pm as per his shift timings. He was thinking of booking his new bike by next month. Till that time he had to rely on taking lifts sometimes from the strangers and sometimes from his office colleagues who are also working in his shift timings. Many a times he rented the shared vehicle till his residence.

One morning as he came to office, he was just checking his normal mails as part of his daily morning office routine and also surfed some news articles. In one of the news articles, he found to his astonishment that last night one of the software guys from another company was robbed of his gold chain and money. It immediately reminded him of similar news few weeks back. For him this came as a new parameter in his ongoing trend of events. This current event of robbery just became a talk of the town and companies started to inform their employees and also took extra security measures for their employees. This incident was a top story for several days in local newspaper and city administration also published some guidelines to be followed by company employees in that area.

After this Bhavesh also thought about the scenario and felt that he should also be allotted a cab service till he buys his own vehicle. It has become a safety threat to travel by private vehicles (either your own or taking lifts from others or a rented vehicle) in the night time. He approached his manager regarding this matter and stated his current concern. He requested Akash to allot him a cab till the time he has his own vehicle. Akash immediately took that in anguish and said that company had already communicated at the time of interview that they would not be providing the cab service. Bhavesh told him that he is aware of that point. But considering the current safety threats, he is requesting for a cab service. Akash said that he will look into the matter. Bhavesh continued by a private rented vehicle for few days and again went to Akash as there was no reply on the cab matter. Akash told Bhavesh that his cab service request has been declined by Senior Manager Pallavi. He won't be able to do anything further in this regard. On this Bhavesh felt this is a genuine concern and should be addressed. He wrote a mail directly to Pallavi requesting and citing the current incidents and published guidelines. Pallavi also didn't replied to his mails despite of several follow ups. He again pinged Akash for the same. This time Akash replied annoyingly that stop sending mails directly, company won't be able to do anything in this regard, "This matter is over". Bhavesh still replied that this service once started could help other executives in the unit.

At this Akash got furious and said "Stop being a social activist and think about your own work. Stop thinking about others. In short, mind your own business". In further discussions he immediately threatened Bhavesh that if he tried to take this matter further(to higher authority) or discussed this further then he would fire him in one single day by putting any allegations like sending a wrong mail to the client etc. Bhavesh was really disappointed as nobody was listening or taking care of his current concern. He felt a little frustrated and thought of giving it up. He thought if our immediate managers are behaving in such a rude manner then whom should we put our concerns to. Then he discussed with his friends who suggested that go as per Akash's advice as he is your immediate manager. Somebody gave a clue that he could take this matter to Ajay sir (Director). Bhavesh was now frightened as Akash had given a direct job threat. He still went to Ajay sir and discussed the matter. Ajay sir within seconds got the feel that this is a genuine concern and should be attended immediately. He approved and arranged a cab for Bhavesh. Now Akash was burning from inside and from next day onwards he started bullying Bhavesh in the ways he could. He asked Bhavesh to get his approval on all mails before sending it to the client. He also started checking his earlier mails. He used to bully him daily in the meeting and would say that he is sending wrong information to the clients. Daily he used to check one of his earlier mails for any faults. He started to find ways to fire Bhavesh. Bhavesh thought it is almost over for him, but he still went through those gruesome and humiliating mail checking sessions. Akash could not find any faults in his earlier proposal to clients. Bhavesh was doing fairly well in achieving his quarterly targets. His performance was really exceptional in this quarter where he has achieved 125% results. His previous quarter performance was also very good where he achieved 100% targets. Work wise Bhavesh was really doing good and Akash was not able to find any faults in his previous work.

As his new strategy, he started to sideline Bhavesh from other executives in his team. This became really embarrassing for Bhavesh. He had no other option but to fight this battle. He continued to do so. Bhavesh wanted to spent atleast a year in the company. He did not want to show less than a year's experience in his resume. Otherwise he could have left the company then and there. More so he felt it a fight against injustice. He wanted to pursue this till end no matter what the outcome is. Challenge has become two fold for Bhavesh now. Since he now has to tackle this harassment at work and also had to focus on achieving his targets. He did not want to give any more chance to Akash.

One day as Bhavesh came to office, Akash called him up in his cabin and informed him that he would have to work in night shift from next week. Bhavesh was not ready to take this as he had done some quality work in past eight months and he is achieving his quarterly targets more than expected.

Akash asked him to transfer his knowledge (K.T.) to other person and to start in night shifts immediately. This is when Bhavesh wrote that long mail to all the company and division heads as he felt that Akash is working in anguish just to throw him out. In this mail he requested senior Head of the Departments to take concern of this matter. Here he also disclosed the feelings of other team members and some of the reason that everybody feels for company's inability to get more clients in the recent client fair held in Dubai. Executives did their work fairly well and had sent the meeting schedules to Akash. But he did not forward them to the concerned person who attended the fair on their division's behalf. Nobody is taking note of this. He has also pointed out to check/investigate this matter. These were some of the last bows in his quiver and Bhavesh did not know what to do next.

His only hope is the meeting that he will have next week with division head in Germany.

Bhavesh is a meditator and often goes to Vipassana meditation centre for practicing.

His friend Rajveer who shares apartment with him asks Bhavesh, "what is the matter"?.

"You appear to be a little depressed, Is there anything going on at workplace"? he asks Bhavesh. At this Bhavesh tells him the whole office saga that has been going on for some time. Rajveer finds this an honest crusade and supported him. He says this has become a trend in the corporate these days. Either live by their terms or leave. He insisted Bhavesh that he should not give up and should continue to raise his concern.

Bhavesh also was over and felt that he would have to either do the night shifts or had to resign.

His subsequent meetings did not do much and the outcome was not that favorable. All the seniors took Akash's side and transferred Bhavesh to night shifts. Bhavesh felt frustrated to the extreme. He thought he would not be able to leave the company before one year and even Akash is taking advantage of this fact. He felt cheated and wanted to throw his venom out.

One day when he was going to his apartment he took a pebble from the ground and hit it towards a broken clay pot lying in the garbage corner.

Immediately he was struck with an idea to take his revenge on Akash. Fight against injustice has now become personal. In this fist of fury he executed the idea.

He thought of making a website named "PaapKaGhada.com". He registered the domain name immediately and started working on website as a freelancer. He thought of showing a pot with the person's name and image caricature[18] on it. The visitor can leave comment and can throw a pebble in the pot. When pebbles crossed more than a threshold hit number, pots water will spill. At this an alert will pop up on the screen stating "Dooms day - PaapKaGhada[19] has filled". It will also register the number of pebbles thrown at that pot.

This was a little rebellious idea but he thought of it as war against injustice. He made this website within three days with the help of Rajveer an HTML(Hyper Text Markup Language)/CSS(Cascading Style Sheet)[20] expert.

Now they use to advertise this through word of mouth. Slowly and gradually people got to know about this website and it became an instant hit amongst the corporate employees. They all got a chance to take their venom out. Website also showed a dashboard with a top pebble hits. Akash's caricature started to top the charts on this website.

Employees started to use this even during the meetings with managers. They use to hit even at the time of meetings just to throw their animosity out(using their smart phones).

This became an instant hit and some senior managers even used this information for appraisals and knowing the acceptability of their new managers. This became a tool in disguise.

This continued for many months. Bhavesh in night shift also use to hit Akash many times.

One Sunday Bhavesh went to a meditation camp and there he met a young entrepreneur. Entrepreneur shared his thoughts with him and told him about this website. Bhavesh hesitated in the start to tell him that it is he who has created this one. Entrepreneur told him that whoever created this site is not doing a good work as it is increasing the animosity further and also

---

[18]   A **caricature** is a rendered image showing the features of its subject in a simplified or exaggerated way.

[19]   **Paap Ka Ghada** is an hindi language word which means "sinners pot" in english

[20]   **HTML** (the Hypertext Markup Language) and **CSS** (Cascading Style Sheets) are two of the core technologies for building Web pages. HTMLprovides the structure of the page, CSS the (visual and aural) layout, for a variety of devices.

creating a divide amongst employees and managers. Sometimes managers and seniors had to take some steps for proper functioning. He said it is solving one purpose but defeating other. He said the person who has such behavior is also a human and might have faced some issues in his life due to which he has acquired the current working style. Not all are wrong; it is just because of few ones the whole pond is corrupted.

This is not the solution. Bhavesh was listening to him quietly as nobody till now has given such a perspective on this situation.

Entrepreneur said instead of hitting that with pebble, we can pray for him "Get well soon" and should give our good wishes as he needs it more. This thought immediately stuck with Bhavesh and he decided to change the websites name to "Maitri Ka Ghada[21]" and the pebbles are now prayer pebbles. Alert now shows as "Get well soon. We give our good wishes to you".

Bhavesh made this change and people now typing the URL "PaapKaGhada.com" are now redirected to "MaitriKaGhada.com". People accepted this one as well.

Entrepreneur also casually visited the site few days later and was surprised to see the changes he suggested to that guy in meditation centre. He could not remember his face but thought that our youth listens to good advice and is a responsible youth.

Meanwhile word got out that Bhavesh made this site and Pallavi and other senior managers called him and thanked him for pointing the discrepancies in the work culture. They said they are working on the possible shuffling for attending the current complaints. Akash finally got a transfer to a new division as there were some other complaints against him as well. Some of the problems are really deep rooted in the subconscious mind which takes their own time to get uprooted but the solution always has a start point however small it may be. Bhavesh quest was a single step in this direction.

Bhavesh is still working in the same division and was promised by Pallavi to move to day shift in the coming quarter.

He does his work fast and writes stories in the rest of the time at night.

Bhavesh is a business development executive by night and also a story writer by night. He is still waiting to see the day light but has paved the way for many.

- By Entrepreneur based on his interaction with Bhavesh, with whom he shares a cordial relationship.

---

[21] MaitriKaGhada is an hindi language word which in English means "Pot of Merits"

Note: His first story named "PaapkaGhada ya MaitriKaGhada" which he co-wrote with entrepreneur on his personal incident became an instant hit amongst the youth employees.

Be Happy
Bhavatu Sabba Mangalam

*** Shree Ganesh ***

KEEP GOING, KEEP MOVING
HAVE FAITH IN MOTHER NATURE

Bhavatu Sabba Mangalam
Deepak

A "Change" Beggar

An old beggar is sitting by the roadside a little away from the main signal. He looks like as if he is not happy from his life. Poverty could easily be inferred from his current state. He is about 70 years old and has a wrinkled face. He has only one pair of clothes and a jute mat with two folds. He uses this mat to sit by the road side. He also has an umbrella which protects him from the broad day sun light. He keeps his change under the mat folds sometimes. He was sitting there asking for alms begging from the visitors passing by - "Please give some change on god's name", he was frequently repeating as if it is coming from his subconscious. This sentence has become a daily practice and a kind of daily ritual for him. This habit is too old to be changed now. He never picks up the change till the end of the day. So passersby can see the change on his jute mat. Now daily passer's by recognizes him and offer him change of either 50 paisa coin or 1 rupee coins. Since the people can see the coins at his jute mat, they often call him a "change beggar". Sometimes he had good collection of coins at the end of the day but some days are not that well. This money was just enough to feed him daily and hardly any savings are done. He is alone and passes his life in despair. People have sometimes seen him talking to himself as if he is complaining to somebody.

One fine day he observes a small boy of around 5-6 years of age standing just nearby his jute mat. He looks at the boy who was staring in amazement at his coin collection. Old man asks his name. Boy does not respond to him. He does not seem to be a well brought up kid. His clothes were also torn. It seems as if he has not taken any bath since a long time. Boy is really fascinated by the shining coins collected at his mat in this broad day sunlight. Boy sits beside the mat and touches the coins from side. Old man sees this often and smiles at the kid. Now boy very often, sometimes daily visits his place.

One day old man fell ill and could not come to his regular place near signal. Daily passersby could not see him for days. The place was empty. The boy also visited that signal many a times just to have a look at his coin collection. But seeing the empty place without the old man he also went away after spending some time at the signal.

Old man lives in a dilapidated place which looked like an old factory site near railway station. Nobody visits that place any more. It is a very aloof and lonely place. It does not seem to be a very good place to live in. He has a small old room where he generally sleeps and passes most of his time. There is no electricity and he had an old lantern out there for the night. He was really ill these days. He was experiencing frequent cough and his throat seems to have an infection. He needed some care at this time but there is nobody to look after him. He manages to stand up and went to the nearby road side tea stall to have a tea. Tea stall owner asks the old man how he is doing. From his outer appearance, he could make out that the old beggar was not well. He asks him to sit on one of the benches and offers him some free biscuits along with a cup of tea. Just then a group of monks came there and just sat on the nearby benches behind the old beggar. A discussion started among the monk meditators about enlightenment and one of the senior monk said that guru has advised that we need to complete our 10 parmis[22] for the enlightenment. One of the young meditators asks the senior one "What did he mean by Parmis"? He explained that "parmis" are like earthen pots, we need to fill them drop by drop. Old man was also listening to them very keenly. This caught his attention. While sitting at the bench he listened to their full conversation. Senior monk explained that these 10 pots are pots of virtues and we need to fill these pots drop by drop with our deeds across different lifetimes. The life span in which these are completed, one gets enlightened. The senior monk named these "parmis" one by one:

1: Generosity
2: Morality
3: Renunciation
4: Wisdom
5: Energy
6: Patience
7: Truthfulness
8: Determination
9: Loving Kindness
10: Equanimity

Old man was listening to this conversation very carefully. The monks left the tea stall after having tea. Old man was still there thinking about the

---

[22] **pāramī** (*Pāli*) is "perfection" or "completeness. The **pāramīs** refer to the perfection or culmination of certain virtues.

discussion. Immediately he had a severe cough with blood this time. The tea stall owner saw this and came running towards him. He gave him warm water to drink. He advised the old man that he should take some medicines. He suggested that he can visit the district government hospital. He told him that it is nearby from this place and he will get some free medicines there. Old man took his advice and left for the hospital.

The road to hospital was a little busy one with the hustle and bustle of the local vegetable market on one side and several poultry shops and the general stores on the other side. The road was always crowded mainly because of the vegetable market. Several small carrier vehicles were parked loading fresh vegetables for other city markets. This was the biggest local vegetable market in city. Old man was walking slowly alongside the road towards the hospital. He managed to cross the vegetable market and other local shops and as he was about to go further, he stumbles on and hits a man accidently with his shoulders. This man was buying different types of diyas and other clay items from the local pottery shop. As a result, some of the diya's fell on the ground and got broken. Diya's[23] were mostly popular at the time of festival of Diwali. Festival was approaching and several people were buying the diya's and other clay items. The man scolds him that "Don't you have eyes" in a harsh tone. Old man feels embarrassed and says sorry to the person. He did not do it intentionally. And slowly walks ahead. This was a hard day for him. He was feeling very low from inside. Further on the route amidst the heavy traffic he crossed a small canal bridge and finally reaches the hospital. He gets himself diagnosed at the hospital and doctors prescribe him with some medicines for his cough related problem. He gets the medicine and walks back to his old factory room.

He felt a little relieved after taking medicine and visits the tea stall owner for thanking him. He now occasionally visits the tea stall for a casual talk. He sees a friendship growing with that tea stall owner and start feeling him as a close friend. He continued with the medications and slowly after some days he felt better and again started going to his usual begging spot in the city. As usual boy also came that day looking for him and was surprised to see the old man there. He came nearby and asked, "Why did he not come to this place for past many days"? He had a tone which appeared as if he is really worried

---

[23] **Diya** is an oil lamp, usually made from clay, with a cotton wick dipped in ghee or vegetable oils. Clay diyas are often used temporarily as lighting for special occasions such as festival of diwali in india.

about the old man. He tells the old man that he used to visit almost daily but got worried after not finding him. "Are you well?" asks the boy. Old man smiles and says nothing. Boy sits for some time and leaves the place.

Old man now leaves the spot a little early each day and started to visit other places in the city for alms begging. He was getting good alms these days.

He used to go to that vegetable market road very often (leaving few days in between). He used to sleep at his room floor peacefully these days. This continued for several weeks and he now has some more begging spots in the city. Now he looks at the daily alms after reaching the home with a peculiar eye as if these are very important ones and he goes for a peaceful sleep after that.

Boy visits the city signal spot very often and shares a word with old man. Old man seems to be little happy these days.

One day as old man comes to his regular city spot and as he was getting ready to settle there, he saw that the young boy was looking at a cycle through a cycle showroom window. Old man sees that by chance. Young boy comes to him after some time and sits beside him on the jute mat. As usual he spent some time there and leaves the old man.

This day old man after reaching his residence looks at today's change and walks towards the top corner and puts his change in the last pot. He had 10 pots there which he has bought from pottery shop at the hospital road.

All the 10 pots are named after 10 parmis and he has been filling them with alms (coin change) collected during the past days. He decided this after listening to those monks at tea stall. As he has been falling ill quite often; he thought of filling his pots quickly. He visited the pottery shop and bought small clay pots over several weeks and named those after the parmis. He looks at the pots with a feeling of satisfaction and content. He sees that all others are full now except the last one with label "Generosity". He has an intention of filling that last one as quickly as possible and puts today's change in it. He could see that it will requires some more days and should be filled with 2-3 more days of alms begging down the lane. He started feeling excited at the thought of completing this job of filling the pots.

He left the next day in hope of getting some good alms. As he reached the city signal spot and opened his mat and umbrella, people started to put "change" at his mat. As the change grew in count, he began to feel happy. He could visualize his last pot getting filled gradually. Just then he again gets a blood cough and this time a severe one. At the same time boy also reached there and becomes worried about the old man. Boy helps him in getting the blood cleaned. He leaves for his house that day with the help of boy.

Next day he takes rest at his room and looks towards the last pot which is still lacking some coins. He thinks that he would be able to make it the next day and will go for alms begging at his regular city signal spot.

Two days later he was sitting at his mat and saw the young boy coming towards him on a small child cycle. As he looked towards the young boy on the cycle he gets a severe cough with blood pouring out. Immediately after that his face hits the change collected in today's alms. People along the roadside gathers around him and sees that old man is no more. Young boy comes to him and starts to weep at the sight. He weeps profusely and misses the old man very much.

After this police arrives at the sight and contacts the tea stall owner near his living place. Tea stall owner tells police about the old man's living place. As police moves inside and searches the house they find 10 empty pots with different names written over them. They could not make out the reason of these empty pots.

Young boy often visits that beggar's signal spot on his cycle. He prays for the old man's soul and thanks him for the gift "The cycle".

Be Happy
Bhavatu Sabba Mangalam

THE WHITE HORSE WARRIOR (BHATONE WALE BABA)

He is coming down from the staircase and the drawing room clock hands are inferring the time to be 10:30 pm. It is night time and he is getting ready to attend one urgent issue at his company. Sometimes back he got a call from his company's customer care about the fix he needs to deliver urgently. He works in a software company and sometimes had to attend these urgent night shift issues. He takes his bike out from parking and starts it. He switches on the headlight but it does not light up. He tries one or two times but it does not light up even then. "There is some problem with the headlight", he senses. He twists the throttle to speed up the engine and cruises towards the company. As he takes a right turn towards the main highway he feels a kind of silence around that has never been experienced by him. There is no traffic at this late hour. It is the month of December and is getting little cold in the absence of moonlight. Some initial part of the highway road is covered by wild bushes on both the sides. However today it appears to be more secluded and alone due to the absence of any traffic. In this dead dark night, it has become even more difficult for him to cross this initial lonely stretch without headlights. He wants to go slowly but has a sense of hurry as well. The city buildings start just after this part is crossed.

He preferred to rent an apartment a little outside for two reasons first it came a little cheap rent wise and it was a bungalow apartment with a private garden. He preferred this apartment as compared to all his friends who preferred the city flats near the company premises. He loves nature and wants to live it fully.

He has still not crossed that initial stretch and was extra cautious while driving today. He was driving swiftly when suddenly he sensed something near his ear. He could hear a strange breezy voice. The wind was not blowing today but still he could sense this windy voice. He turned his neck little towards left and saw nothing. A little anxiety took over and his heart started to pump a little fast as if falling short of the blood supply. He kept calm and continued driving. Again after some time he sensed the same voice near his right ear this time. He didn't want to look back but slowly turned his neck towards right side keeping an eye on the front road as well. As he turned towards right the noisy voice was gone. He continued but his heart has started pounding a little fast by now. After some time again a voice came towards his left ear and this time his bike all of a sudden started to slow down. He could not understand and continued for some more time. By then bike got really slow and he sensed it got punctured. He stopped by road side. He is in middle of nowhere, no street lights, no moonlight, no headlight and it was total darkness around. As he was standing there he saw a strange figure emerging out of air approaching towards him. It had no legs just the above part of the body. It had a little shine similar to moonlight but he could not see the face part clearly. He saw that entity moving very fast just few steps ahead of him almost crossing at the front of his face. He got frightened and started to run in the bushes. As he ran he saw that figure approaching towards his back and he continued running. He was running with sweat on his face. He could very distinctly hear his breath in that dark night. He stopped after some time and tried to look back. As he turned he saw the figure standing at his back. He ran again and reached an old pond with a stone wall on one side. He was just about to jump in the pond but immediately he stopped as if somebody is calling him from back. He didn't know what to do and he ran alongside the pond now. He entered the village by the pond side and continued running among the houses. Suddenly he felt a strong pull towards one of the village house. He jumped and ran upstairs towards the first floor. As he reached at the first floor he could not find anybody there but did not feel like waiting there also. Suddenly he fell on the first floor veranda and saw the same figure appearing in his front. He was shaken to his deepest roots. He felt a strong surge through the spine. He thought he would live no more and his end is near. The figure disappeared all of a sudden and he heard the same voice calling him again as heard by him near the pond. He didn't know what to do but felt attracted towards this voice. He came downstairs and started to run again when suddenly at a few meters distance he saw two persons standing calmly as if waiting for him. One person was wearing white clothes and other had a big moustache. The person with white clothes pulled him in his sweet shop. The other one was a barber in that area. They said that they have come from place called "Bhatone" (near Gulaothi in Bulandshahr district of Indian State of Uttar Pradesh). After a while one of them went outside and came on his white horse. The barber took the back seat and pulled him in between them. They were now protecting him from the entity.

As they were about to leave, I got up from my sleep. It was a terrifying dream and I felt the sweat all over my face. I was still terrified in my bed. I looked outside the window there was no moonlight. It was a dark night. I was alone and my body was shaking in fear. Immediately I looked for and found one photo of my spiritual guru and kept that by my bedside. I felt little relieved after that and didn't remember when I fall asleep again.

Next morning I called up my father and narrated the whole dream incident as if it is happening live in front of my eyes. Father kept quiet for some time and then said they must be our family clan protector. He then told me about "The White Horse Warrior" who lived in a village near our ancestral village area in 1700 AD. His name was Sahaj Ram. He was a very humble person and use to help people in and around the village. He loved white color very much and always used to wear white clothes with a white turban. He had a white female horse as his companion. People often have seen him riding on it. Everyone in that area knew him as a protector. Due to his protecting and helping nature, he became very famous person in the nearby village areas. My father told me that other person might be his friend. He said that there are some ancient stories about him as well which generally is the point of discussion many a times in the village gatherings. But very less is documented about him.

After hearing about his story from my father, I felt a deep sense of gratitude for him and his friend. It was really a dark night for me. The incident still ran in front of my eyes. I decided to visit his place of Samadhi and got the address from my father.

I took a week's leave from my office and went to my home town. I stayed there for about two days and then left for his village. I boarded a bus till the village. It took around 2-3 hours from my home town. I left the bus at the outskirts of the village and rested a while at a small tea stall just outside the village area. I asked the tea stall owner about "The White Horse Warrior" Samadhi place. He guided me and said that it will take a while from here and you can either take a bullock cart or go by foot. He told that if you are planning to take a walk till there, then do ask in between from other people about the route as there are some turns in between. I thanked him and carried on my foot for some time. I saw a turn and there was nobody around to guide me. I took a turn as per my guess and continued treading that path. After walking for some time, I could not see any turn and there were lonely crop fields till the far end. I stopped for a while and thought," I might have taken a wrong turn". Immediately, I saw a person coming from the opposite direction. I asked him about the Samadhi place. He told me that, "you have taken a wrong turn" and said that he is also going to the same place. He can follow him till there. I turned back and followed him. In the meanwhile I chatted with him about the village and about the "The White Horse Warrior" stories. He shared quite a few stories with me. He seems to be an old person. I got engrossed while talking to him and did not realize how my journey was covered. Finally I saw a right turn in front of me with a small board at the corner. The board has - "The white Horse warrior Samadhi place this way" written over it. Old man took that turn and I followed him towards the Samadhi. This seems to be a busy and crowded route as I could see many devotees going towards his Samadhi. As I reached the Samadhi mandir(temple); I saw people moving towards the main gate. There was a place in the centre where people used to lit the diya's[24] and on one side I saw a big hand-made wall drawing of a person sitting on a white horse. As I saw that picture I immediately turned back to look for that old village man. It exactly resembled that old man. But I could not find him anywhere, he was gone. I stood there for some time and realized that he showed me the correct path one more time. A deep gratitude for him arose from my heart. After waiting there for a while I entered the temple premises and lit a diya for him and my family's good will. I left the place with some more stories which the old villager narrated on the way. Hoping to write them one day....

Bhatone Wale Baba – Bless me and my family. Bless us all.

Be Happy
Bhavatu Sabba Mangalam

---

[24] **Diya** is an oil lamp, usually made from clay, with a cotton wick dipped in ghee or vegetable oils. Clay diyas are often used temporarily as lighting for special occasions such as festival of diwali in india.

MICKEY: THE GIRL WITH AN "AUM" TAATOO

Ravi has arrived from Sydney to meet his family. His flight landed this morning at Mumbai airport. All through his journey a thought of good story has clouded his mind in this cloudless weather outside. He wanted to start with a short animation movie but the right story concept has not clicked him till now. All his conscious attempts to come up with a story have failed till now. He has been thinking about the same for quite some time. He really wants to make his mark in the world of animation. After coming out of the airport, he hired a private cab to city of Pune. Ravi is an arduous devotee of lord Shiva and thinking of a vacation in Leh-Laddakh (Mount Kailash). He was planning to visit his parents from quite a while now. He has come to India to meet his parents almost after a year. Several years back he immigrated to Australia. Before that he used to work as a visual effect supervisor in one of the film studios in Mumbai, India. While working there he applied for a Supervisor role in a big Visual Effects studio in Sydney and got a decent offer from the company. He is living a settled life in Sydney these days.

He reached his Pune apartment safely. As he rang the door bell his mother came to open the door. He could see a heart touching smile on her face which only a child can understand. She got very emotional seeing him after a year. His father also came there and he greeted both of them by touching their feet.

His mother and father live alone and they are really worried about his marriage. They want him to get married as soon as possible and get settled now. They are trying hard to get a suitable match for Ravi. They have shortlisted some of the probable ones for him. They want Ravi to meet them before they could go ahead. Ravi will give the final yes before proceeding ahead with the marriage proposal. It would be an arranged marriage. They were anxiously waiting for Ravi's trip this year and hoping that they will able to find a suitable match for him. After taking some rest Ravi meets his father at dining table during the evening tea. His father asks his mother to bring some of the recent photographs. He shows him few photographs but still finds Ravi very reluctant towards marriage. They are completely unaware of the thoughts that are hovering Ravi's mind at this point of time. Marriage is the least of the priority for him now. He first of all wants to set up his own animation production house. He has been trying hard to get the right story for starting his first animation movie but all his efforts till now have achieved nothing.

Nothing is really working for him. Though he has got all comforts but his ambitions are somewhere else. This is the main reason that Ravi is avoiding all the marriage discussions at home. He feels that a small vacation will give him some time off. Ravi has an old friend named Santosh in Mumbai, who is working as a Visual Effects (VFX) supervisor in one of the Mumbai's film studios. They both were working in the same company before Ravi's immigration. Santosh decided to stay here and Ravi immigrated to Sydney, Australia. He calls up Santosh after a long time. He has his old phone number and thinks if he would be able to reach him over the call. Phone rings and he hears him after a long time.

"Hello, Who is it on the other side?" Santosh says in his signature tone.

Ravi is really happy to hear him after so long and replies "Ravi here".

Santosh also remembers his tone and says "What a surprise. Where are you calling from"?

Ravi answers that he is in Pune currently and has come to meet his parents. The discussion continued and they shared some good old past memories. Ravi was not in touch with him for past two years. So it was a pleasant surprise for him. They talk over phone and Ravi asks him if he can join him for a small vacation in Himalayas. Santosh find this as a good way for a get together trip. He has not that much work load in his office these days. But he cannot confirm it right away, so he replies that "He needs to inquire about the vacation and will have to ask his boss for the leave tomorrow". If his boss agrees then he can come along. Ravi is positive about this and waits for his call. Santosh finally gets the approval from his boss and they plan a small vacation to Himalayas, Leh-Laddakh. Ravi does all the bookings and hotel arrangements. His parents are worried to find his disinterest in marriage proposals. His father decides to talk to him personally regarding this matter. Just then, Ravi tells them about the trip and the plan for the discussion is delayed once again. But his father is really adamant this time. He is really interested to know about his mindset.

They leave for Himalayas and visits Mount Kailash. They were awestruck looking at Mount Kailash at early morning hours. They took some snaps of mount Kailash at about 3 am in the morning. The snaps were amazing. Later, they forwarded the same on their social networking messaging client. The snaps were highly appreciated by everyone in the group. Some of the group members even wondered that they seem "Out of the world". They were true about the snaps. Mount kailash's beauty in those pictures was immeasurable. It was also the auspicious day of Mahashivratri (the day of Lord Shiva). Ravi used to fast on this day each year.

On return journey he pays a visit to a local Shiva temple. All through this journey the thought of a good story was bogging him down. This thought was always there at the back of his mind. Whenever he wanted to forget this, it gets surfaced and used to knock his conscious mind again. All his conscious attempts to come up with a story have failed till now. He went inside the temple gate and walks till the white Shivling[25] at the centre of the temple. He bows down to lord Shiva and started weeping there for some time. Tears came naturally in his eyes. All his burning ambitions just passed through his mind with in a flash. He surrenders all his ambitions to Lord Shiva and raises his head to stand up. He thinks by now "Whatever he has started, is not working". He always wanted to have his own animation production house. He wishes good health for his family and prays for everyone. He bows his head again and put his offering in donation box. The temple priest watches him and offers him two prasadam packets. He keeps the packet in his handbag and returns with his eyes still wet. Santosh who was standing at a distance behind him asks "Why his eyes are so wet, what's the matter"? He looks towards him and says nothing.

After that, they take the return journey back to Pune and reaches home after about three days. His parents are delighted to see him again. He was a bit tired and immediately goes to his room for some rest. Santosh due to some urgency at his office has left to Mumbai without even visiting his parents. Next morning Ravi looks for his phone in his handbag. He sees two prasadam packets there. He wanted to hand over one of them to Santosh but he is not here, so takes both of them to his parents. His mother takes one and asks him to take the other one along with him to Sydney. He prepares his luggage for the flight scheduled for day after tomorrow. He will leave for Sydney in coming two days. He keeps the prasadam packet at the end. He knew that he was on a short visit this time and most of the time was occupied in his Mount Kailash visit. His parents are still thinking of his marriage especially his father but he refrains from any further talks.

Two days later, he leaves for airport in the morning. His father is driving him to the airport. His father really wants to know his marriage plans. He

---

[25] **Shivling** is a representation of the Hindu deity Shiva used for worship in temples. In traditional Indian society, the Sivling is rather seen as a symbol of the energy and potential of God, Shiva himself.

feels that Ravi is well settled and it is the right time to get married. His father had sensed back at home that he is ignoring the discussion and is not answering promptly. He wanted him to discuss it openly. He asks if there is some one of his choice in Sydney do let us know. After this, first time he opened up and said no dad, it's nothing like that. They were moving towards Mumbai airport via Pune-Mumbai expressway. As they were crossing the ghats[26] they saw there was a huge traffic jam ahead. They also got stuck there but could do nothing about it. They planned to reach before time but now they are stuck in traffic jam. At this time his father continued the discussion about his plans. Ravi said that he wants to get settled first. Father asked "Aren't you settled now"? He said yes in a way I am but I have some other ambitions in the field of animation and they are eating up his current focus. He discusses in detail about his future ambitions and plans. Father said you can continue that even after marriage but he replied that he wanted to setup his business first. Father looks at his watch in between and realises that they are getting late to airport. Jam began to clear up slowly and they also got out from traffic jam. His father looked at his wrist watch again and pressed the accelerator a little more as if the watch has given him the green signal. He was conscious of them getting late and started driving very fast. Ravi had never seen his father driving like this before. His father was totally focusing on driving now as he also felt that the discussion has come to a saturation point. So it was a kind of silence inside and they did not talk much after that. His father drove fast and tried his best but still he was an hour late. They reached the airport and the car stopped just outside the departure terminal gate. Ravi gets out in a sense of hurry and pulls the luggage trolley very fast. He puts the luggage on the trolley and runs towards the entry gate.

Ravi is aware that he is very late and enters the gate at the last minute. He looks back at his dad who is waiting for him to say good bye. Ravi smiles and waves his hand. His dad replies with a smile and says "God Bless You my Son; Take Care" and drives the car away from the entry gate. Just outside the main entry gate the airport police check Ravi's Identity card. Mickey is feeling ok on the sugar hills inside the prasadam card board packet. She has nothing to do, she never loses hope. She is always ready for the life adventures. He shows his passport and moves inside after the Identity card verification. He moves inside the airport with his entire luggage on the trolley. She is feeling some jerks inside. The luggage bag is on the trolley now. He is walking very fast

---

[26] **Ghat** is a mountain pass.

almost running with the luggage trolley. The luggage is on the roll so there are ad-hoc jerks inside. He has even skipped his final call at the airport so he is in a real rush. He stands in the queue in haste as he was already late for the check in. He runs for the counter which was now empty but he still has to cross the barricade maze which was placed there just to control the flow of passengers in line. There are no passengers now and he rushes with fury towards the counter taking left and right turns through the maze. She feels a sudden roller-coaster ride inside. She is lively and takes everything in her own stride. He reaches at the counter and asks for the check in. The girl at reception very politely asks him to move towards the supervisor counter. "The counter is closed now", she says. He insists her for the check-in but she refuses and requests him for moving to the next supervisor counter. Ravi accepts that and moves towards the next counter with his luggage trolley. He sees a fat lady sitting over there.

Yes gentleman "How can I help you"?, lady asks Ravi.

He says he needs to check-in for the Sydney flight. Supervisor lady says you are already late. Ravi shivers a little. She says you can check in but we will send your luggage with the next flight. On hearing this Ravi gets a little irritated and says what he is going to do without luggage. It has to go with him. "Do something about it", he requests her. She says the conveyer belt for carrying the luggage is too long and will take much time. By that time your flight will already take off. Ravi insists again and says that he will not leave without luggage. She should cooperate in such emergency hours. On this the fat lady says ok gentleman I will take your luggage and if it does not reach with this flight then you should inquire about it in the next flight. She examines his ticket and passport and hands over his boarding pass. Ravi thanks her for considering his case. Now Ravi leaves the counter in much haste almost running towards the security counter. His luggage is on the conveyer belt moving swiftly towards the aircraft. She feels as if it's a smooth ride after such a roller coaster one. He goes through the full security check and moves towards the final check at customs. After getting a stamp here on his passport and boarding pass he almost runs for the flight boarding gate in east block. The block is yet quite far but he has no other option. The way to east block gate has many private snacks counter on both the sides. The crowd is full as it is an international airport. He finally finds his boarding gate and checks at the desk. Young lady there examines his boarding pass and allows him in. He walks in to the sloping way attached to the airplane's main gate. He was the last one to enter the plane. He feels a little relaxed after this much exciting run and chase sequence. He finally sits on his seat and puts his hand bag in the cupboard above him. He eases out a little but is still little worried about the luggage and prays to Lord Shiva. The flight takes off and everything settles down after the initial briefing about the flight safety measures by the air hostesses from the flight crew. He takes a sleep and flight sails towards Sydney. She is alone inside and there is much darkness around. She takes it casually as she has complete faith in Mother Nature. Her motto in life can be summarized in one line "Keep going, keep moving. Have faith in mother nature". She utilizes her time and sits there in deep meditation. She remained in deep meditation even during the intermediate flight stops.

Ravi has a smooth and safe flight to Sydney. Flight reaches there about approximately 20 hours later. He comes out of the plane and moves towards the conveyer belt for the luggage. He is ready to wait there patiently as his luggage was the last one. All passengers are gathered at the belt with their trolleys. He could see the moving empty conveyer belt. Luggage only started to appear after a wait of 5-10 minutes. He was looking at the airport hoardings when he sees his luggage at the front. He is surprised to see that his luggage is the first one on the conveyer belt. He had not expected that at all. He thinks that may be it is due to the fact that his luggage was the last one to check in. He finds this one as a good algorithm for getting the luggage early "Last in first out". Then he comes forward towards the moving conveyer belt for picking it up. He puts that up on the trolley and moves to the immigration checking point. The lady officer checks in the passport and puts a stamp on it. He walks out of the airport and looks for cab towards the city. He hires a private cab to his duplex apartment. By now, she also comes out of his meditation and feels a new air. He reaches his apartment after some time and opens the main gate. He has a rented apartment in the heart of Sydney. He looks at the swastika sign attached at the centre of the main gate. He enters inside and keeps his luggage at the side and moves towards the wash basin just outside the wash room. He freshens up a bit and relaxes for some time.

Ravi gets up after an hour and opens his luggage for changing his clothes. He opens up and finds the prasadam[27] packet at the top. He puts that on the dining table and looks for his apparels. After changing he goes to the dining table and opens the prasadam box and picks up one piece. Mickey is

---

[27]   **Prasad** (Hindustani pronunciation: [prəsaːd̪]; also called **prasada** or **prasadam**) is a material substance of food that is a religious offering in both Hinduism and Sikhism. It is normally consumed by worshippers. 'Prasad' literally means a gracious gift. It denotes anything, typically an edible food, that is first offered to a deity, saint, Perfect Master or an avatar, and then distributed in His or Her name to their followers or others as a good sign.

somewhere hiding on the side which Ravi is unable to see. He enjoys it and relaxes in the main bedroom. In the meantime Mickey is feeling little relaxed after a long meditation session. She wants to have a fresh air. This is when she gets out from prasadam box and walks down the table corner to move over the table leg towards the floor. She is not familiar with such an up market and sophisticated premises. She has always lived in open spaces. As she walks down the floor she could see some light coming from the bottom of the back gate. She leaves the card board box and let herself loose towards the balcony. She moves outside from under the back door to see a beautiful garden with many trees. At her first glance she observes a big mango tree at one side of the garden. There is a green hedge just protecting that and other flower plants. She walks and crosses the grass and other holy basil plants in between to walk over the bricks row under the hedge.

As she climbs the brick row and comes down on the inside she sees a lot of soldier ants marching parallel to the hedge as if they are going on a hunt. These ants were much bigger in size than her. As Mickey was coming down she slipped and falls in their way. They stopped and could see Mickey lying down. This was a sudden encounter. She stood there doing nothing. Mickey quickly came on to her foot. One of the bull dog ants came forward to bully her. This is the first face off and bulldog ants were about to kill her when Jackey the male soldier ant comes forwards for her rescue. Mickey never gives up and now stands face to face with a soldier ant with her hands folded. It is now that her "Aum Taatoo" is visible for the first time on the front part of her neck. Jackey the male soldier watches this and was impressed at her guts. She stands face to face with the soldiers without any fear on her face with both her hands folded in cross. Though her height is much less than that of the bull dogs ants but her pride is not. The faceoff was tight. By this time Jackey also reached there for her help. He mediates and tries to ease out the situation a bit by asking about her.

He asked his tribe members to just calm down and let him inquire about her. "Who are you young lady? And where have you come from?" he asked her. You do not seem to be from this neighborhood. She replies in calm demeanor and answers "I am a Himalayan Ant from India and my name is Mickey". And tells that she is here by-chance. The soldiers have heard about the location from the queen "Sheeba" of the tribe. Upon hearing the Himalayan tribe Jackey says leave her alone and takes her in one corner. Others say that you deal with her, we are leaving for the work. He says that "I am Jackey the male soldier of the tribe". He says she can get killed as some of the ants are really killer ants. At this she says nothing and looks straight in his eyes. Jackey sees a confident ant here and asks her to meet their queen. Mickey is unaware of the location and she asks Jackey about the location, "Which location is it"? Jackey replies that you are in Sydney Backyard in front of killer Bull Dog ants. At this Jesse feels a little jealous as Jesse has a soft corner for Jackey. Jesse is one of their tribe members and she likes Jackey very much. She wants to keep Jackey away from Mickey. But Jackey finds a sense of confidence in Mickey despite being small in size than bull dog ants. Jackey feels a strange kind of attraction towards her personality. After the initial conversation, Jackey asks her "Where is she staying"? She replies that, she is here by chance and do not know much about the place. She replies that she will find some place to stay. At this, Jackey offers her to stay with them. She resists as she has just escaped a death bed. They were about to kill her. At this, Jackey shows her a secret place to stay under mango tree just beside the main trunk. She can stay there till the time she gets comfortable with other members of the tribe. Jackey tells her that they live in a nearby hole and will meet her tomorrow morning. She agrees to stay there. Night approaches and she sleeps after this major turning point in her life.

Next day Ravi wakes up and is getting ready for his office. Ravi moves out after taking bath and as he looks outside the window he could see bunch of mangoes on the tree. The tree is full of mangoes this season. He goes outside to pluck the first mango of this season. It is now that Mickey sees Ravi for the first time. Ravi offers the first one to Sun Deity and Lord Krishna in his meditation room. He has not plucked any mangoes in this season till now. Some of them have already ripened (Offering First crop to Sun deity and Lord Krishna is considered auspicious in Indian culture).

Ravi leaves for the office and it is now that Mickey comes to the main garden and roams there for some time. She wants something to eat but could not find anything till now. She searches around and then after sometime she spots a ripened mango lying in one corner under the hedge. She goes there and tries to eat it from one side. Other ants are also there on the other side. She manages to hide herself while eating. In the meantime Jackey comes looking for her and finds her at one side of ripened mango. He says Good Morning to her and Mickey hears and looks down. She smiles back. And then they both eat the mango and share some good moments. Jackey invites her to the evening dinner with the queen. He says that others have already told about you to the queen last night. Queen also wants to meet you and appears really interested to know some of your experiences. Mickey is first hesitant but on Jackey's insistence she agrees to come. Day passes and Jackey come to pick her up and it is the first time she enters their underground tribe. After initial round of discussion Queen asks her to come over and introduce herself to others. She introduces herself that she is an Himalayan ant and is here by chance. She has no tribe here and do not know where to live. Queen notes this and asks her to tell us something about her native place. She tells everybody about the Himalayas and its spiritual significance. She tells them that Himalayas is the spiritual hub of the world. She says Earth's kundalini top chakra is situated there. Queen seems really interested to hear this one. They have a quiet and a serene life there and she also tells them about Himalayan marmots as she lives nearby. She tells them that these huge big creatures lives there and digs the gold mixed sand from their burrows. At this queen gets extra conscious and asks her if she could tell more about the gold part. She says there is not much to it but yes many people have visited their place just in search of gold. Many archaeologist and others excavators have visited that place in the past following that ancient gold myth. In fact they have named these creatures as gold digging ants. Queen really likes this story and finds her vocal/oratory skills very good. She finds a good teacher in her and starts thinking about her role in the tribe. Queen has never done this thing before, as Mickey is not one of their tribes. She decides to wait for some more time before announcing this officially in the tribe. She wanted to see everyone's acceptance about her. They finished the dinner and then queen says keep meeting us. Queen asks her where she is staying these days. She tells about the place under mango tree. "As you are our guest", she asks Jesse to look after her and to let mickey stay with her. Jesse agrees with not so good feeling on her face. They both move at Jesse's place. Jesse also gets a chance to interact with her. This was a nice opportunity for Jesse to know more of her. Day passed and the three form a new gang in tribe.

It's a weekend and Ravi plans to pluck the mangoes for the homemade preparations. Ravi plucks them with the help of a thin iron rod for the ones which are at the top and he plucks the lower ones with his hands. He has a bucket full of mangoes this season and he asks his maid to indulge in the chutney[28]/pickle preparation. He gets busy in figuring/finalizing his animation movie ideas. He is thinking of new ways of generating income. He has invented some story ideas but could not find a convincing one to start his animation movie till now. He meditates daily in the morning before going to office. He daily uncovers the curtain of the window and looks outside before

---

[28] **Chutney** is a family of condiments associated with South Asian cuisine made from a highly variable mixture of spices, vegetables or fruit.

sitting for meditation. It also allows some sunlight in the room. He looks at the mango tree from the window and shares his thanks giving after each meditation session. He could sense the tree showing a happy gesture many a times.

Now Jackey and Mickey are forming a new pair in the tribe. One evening as they were about to leave after a meeting they hear a screaming voice. Ravi's maid screams and asks Ravi to come over. She shows him a small black child snake. Ravi immediately clears him and takes him in the polythene bag to throw outside the house at one side of the garden. Jackey and Mickey gets excited after hearing to their conversation. They also move towards that side of the garden to have a look at little snake. As Ravi comes outside they have already reached at that spot. Ravi drops the snake out of polythene at one side of the garden. They find snake coming towards them and they happen to jump on to him in hurry. Snake also get a little hysterical and starts to move fast. They both were holding on to him very tightly. The snake was circling in between the bricks outside and they both are still sticking to his body. This was a little roller coaster ride for them. They finally loosen the grip and were thrown at a tangent at some distance from his body. It was a fun time for both of them. After this adventurous ride, Jackey says good night and Mickey moves to Jesse place. Jesse asks where she is coming from. She tells her the truth about the snake incident. It's a little unusual for Mickey. She could sense Jesse reactions on this.

Mickey and Jackey generally meet at the same spot where they met for the first time under the tree. They have named it the "Ant Point". While roaming there around the tree they happen to see a ripe mango still intact at the top of the tree. So there is one last ripe mango which both of them are aware of now. But it is at the tree top. "The master has plucked all mangoes and he must be thinking that there are no more left" says Mickey. Mickey and Jackey both tracks that last mango ripening day by day and dreams of a special Sunday brunch one day whenever it falls off.

Few more days pass off and Ravi was sitting in the morning meditation. And just when he opened his eyes after the session he looked at the tree outside the window. It is when he casually spots that last mango on the tree. He thought that he has plucked all of them but now he could see this one, perhaps it was the last of this season. He moves to the garden next day morning but could not find the mango. He tries to search it under the hedge and sees it nowhere in the garden. He then moves inside the hedge and could finally locate it lying just besides the hedge. He sees that there are lots of ants sticking on it. Mickey and Jackey are also onto it having their last feast of the season when master picks it up but then he thinks of something and again keeps it at the same place. After looking at so many ants enjoying it he thinks let the ants eat it completely. He donates the last one to ants generously. This was a close encounter of Mickey with Ravi. She now could remember his face. And he moves inside the house and leaves for the office.

Ravi also has a habit of putting up the sugar cubes just under the mango tree. The ants loved this from their heart. Rainy season has already started and the tree has no mangoes left now. Ants are aware of this fact and indulge themselves in search for the new food source. It's now that the sugar cubes are coming in handy for the ants. Master loves to feed ant and does it as a habit now.

Mickey and Jackey have come closer by now and Mickey plans to give a surprise to Jackey for his help and support in a foreign land. Mickey asks Jackey to come over the next morning under the mango tree at the same place they had met for the first time i.e. "Ant Point". Next morning as Jackey comes; Mickey asks him to close his eyes and open it only when she says it. She reaches the site but could not see it. Jackey says should I open it now. She says ok and is not happy at this. Jackey asks "What is it"? She says nothing and asks him to come next morning. Same thing happens next morning also.

Ravi seems to be a little excited with sudden turn of events. He is closing a small wooden case as if he is keeping something in it. Jackey comes next day and same thing happens next day also. Now Mickey is a little worried and decides to check it herself the next morning. She finds that the ball is getting picked up by Ravi each morning. Ravi is really excited to see the ball in the garden, he seems a little puzzled as if from where are they coming. Ravi is picking up the golden balls from the garden and is keeping them in a secret case inside his puja[29] ghar (place where he keeps all his idols, place where he worships). He is still amazed and puzzled as if from where these golden balls are coming all of a sudden. Mickey watches this and continues to teleport these balls for him. Mickey calls Jackey in the evening time instead of morning time and gives him the surprise with the little golden ball. Jackey is amazed to see the golden ball. He asks her from where she is getting these balls. She tells Jackey that she knows how to teleport things but does not use this always. She is teleporting these balls from the golden dust of the Himalayan gold digging ants. They dig the dust with the golden traces in it.

---

[29] **Puja** (Hinduism) Pūjā is a prayer ritual performed by Hindus to host, honour and worship one or more deities, or to spiritually celebrate an event.

She used to live nearby that place and use to watch them digging. Jackey is amazed to see this ability of hers. He asks her, "How do you know the secret art of teleportation"? It is now she tells the story from her past birth:

"She tells that she was an ant in her previous birth and use to live near a Himalayan cave where a yogi used to live. Yogi used to teach meditation to his pupils. It is during those times that she has learnt the meditation and she practiced in her alone time. As she progressed in meditation one fine day she got the supernatural ability of teleportation. In this birth she has this ability right from the birth. Jackey is a now awestruck with her abilities and thanks her for the gold ball. He asks her, "Is it the same ball that she wanted to show in the morning under the tree". She said yes but why was it not there. She then told about Ravi. She said that Ravi is picking these up from under the tree. She now plans to continue to do that as she think Ravi is in need of that. Jackey ask her to meet the queen of the tribe again. He says queen would be very happy to know about this ability of hers. They meet the queen in the evening and Jackey hands over the golden ball to her. Queen is very happy to see this and then Jackey tells her about Mickey's ability to teleport. Queen is very surprised and she was very really impressed at this. She appoints Mickey as the chief advisor of the tribe. Jackey now loves her more and wants to take some lessons from her to learn about this ability. They both are sitting on the sugar cube which Ravi has put in the morning just under the tree. Ravi seems to be in a happy frame of mind these days. Mickey says to Jackey if you want to learn how to teleport then he must learn first how to meditate. But there is a word of caution. Do not use this for selfish purposes. Also he should be punctual in his daily meditation practice. Jackey gives a positive affirmation on this. Mickey started to teach Jackey how to meditate and they both started meditating on the top of sugar cube and day passed as usual. Jesse feels a little jealous about Mickey considering their closeness these days. Somewhere in her heart she still loves Jackey.

One fine day Mickey is nowhere to be found. Jackey comes at their regular spot next morning and could not find her anywhere. He inquired about her with the Queen. Queen does not have any knowledge about her whereabouts. He asks Jesse but she is also blank. Jackey the lone warrior waits for her at "Ant Point" all day long but she did not come. He tried looking for her at few of their familiar meeting points but could not find her there also. Mickey has teleported herself back to Himalayas in her own tribe. Jackey still waits for her. Jesse is still in love with Jackey. Ravi goes next day and did not find any gold ball there and looks towards the sky. He could not grasp from where these balls were coming. The mystery is still on for him. He goes inside and counts the balls.... He still looks at that spot in the garden each morning.

Once in a while Ravi counts the gold balls in the box. His last count was 108. He does not have any clue yet from where they have appeared in his garden. He thanks Lord Shiva for the same.

Few days later Ravi gets a dream about Mickey the teleport ant and other bull dog ants. He remembers the whole story in the morning and finds it very convincing. He decides to make this as his first animation movie. He dedicates this first movie to Lord Shiva. And names it "Mickey: The Ant with an Aum Tatoo".

Father calls him on the day of movie release and tells him about the marriage proposal. She has done MCA (Masters in Computer Application) and got admission in Sydney University for higher studies. He also feels ok about this proposal.

As per the first hand online reviews the movie is declared as an instant hit among the children's as well as the elders. It has been really appreciated by the viewers. Ravi feels a little relaxed as his production house has finally taken off to a good start and now he can full time work where his heart is.

Next morning he sits in meditation and a genuine gratitude comes towards Lord Shiva. He takes a vacation back home and meets his parents in Pune, India. They show him the girl's photograph. Her name is Parvati. He feels ok and a real gratitude comes towards lord Shiva. He calls up Santosh and they again plan a visit to the same temple where they had first visited. They reach at the temple and he bows down in gratitude at the Shivling. As he bows down Mickey is looking at him from beside the temple. She is having a Trident (Trishul) at her back visible above her right shoulder. She smiles as if the mission is over and disappears.....

Thanks to Lord Shiva – HAR HAR MAHADEV.

BeHappy
Bhavatu Sabba Mangalam

THE BOOT POLISH
ENTREPRENEUR

———◆———

I was sitting on my seat in a train's general compartment heading towards my office in Mumbai. Three men came one by one and occupied the front bench seat. One of them behaved like as if he was not use to this type of crowd. Another one calm and quiet as if looking for someone; third one an age old person as if he is going to meet somebody. Looking at the old men reminded me of the fact that we all are searching for one thing or the other and it appears that the search never ends perhaps. The front bench was fully occupied now and I looked at all of them and my eyes stayed on the middle one where a young man was sitting wearing spectacles. Looking at his clothes he seems to be a well brought off person. Immediately my attention got disturbed by a child's voice literally shouting "Boot Polish" "Boot Polish" and I saw a small kid wearing withered clothes and having a small wooden box in his hands. The old man sitting at front bench asked him "How much?" He replied 10 Rupees for one polish. He said ok. The kid handed over his newspaper to the person and started polishing his leather shoes. This reminded me of Ram a very bright kid whom I had met in one such compartment in my younger days.

"Ram is running very fast towards the railway station to catch his train. As he enters the station premise and started to climb the outer staircase towards the over bridge he takes a pause for a second as if he has forgotten something. He turns back and runs towards one side of the station. He makes it a point to always feed the birds specially pigeons outside railway station. There was an age old stone fountain which is non-functional these days. Beneath it was a regular meeting point for the birds in that area. People use to throw away the grains for feeding the birds. As usual he was wearing one of the two t-shirts with a pigeon image on front side. He threw away the grains in a hurry and said "Ok Bye for today" and runs back towards the platform. On reaching the platform No. 3 he chases fast and runs like anything to catch the train. He has been a little late that day and train has already left for Mumbai from Pune junction. He has reached there at the last minute and he could see the back side of the last general bogey receding away as train paced up to its normal speed. He tried hard to catch but could not succeed. His breath is running very fast. He stood there for some time having his hands rested on his knees, relaxing a bit till his breath came to normal. He saw an empty platform bench towards his left and went to sit there for some time. He kept aside his boot polish wooden box. While resting he thought today's chance has gone and he would have to go to city market in the evening for some earnings. He is 10 years old and boards train two or three times a week for his boot polish work. This way he earns some extra money to meet up his requirements. Rest of the days he generally spends time at local organization which is working for educating underprivileged children's.

He leaves the station and returns to his home. After freshening up for sometime he immediately leaves for today's class. He reaches there a little late and sits in one corner. John sees this with a side eye but continues with the ongoing class. Today he is teaching students basics about the daily book keeping. He is currently focusing on the record keeping of the daily expenditures/earnings/donations and net profit etc. He is teaching children about the positive aspects of book keeping. He believes that book keeping is very important part for every person's day to day activities and people should do the book keeping of their daily expenses/earnings. It gives them a good start and overview in their money management skills. It helps them in curtailing the unnecessary expenses. He knows that these kids have a long way to go but he still feels that this initial training will help them immensely in whatever they do. He did not wish for them but could easily see that some of them will get involved in child labor. So ultimately the organization is trying to make some contributions in improving their future. John is from United Kingdom and is now staying in Pune working for this organization. He is also a language teacher and works with these young kids in improving their English speaking skills. Ram attends the class and john asks after the class "What happened, you came today"? Ram answered that he missed the train by seconds so he thought it would be good to attend the class instead. John knows that Ram is a very bright student but he also has his own set of responsibilities. He has an ailing mother whom he had to look after. John sees a bright spark in Ram. Ram is one of the best kids in his class. Ram also finds John's advice very useful and is really getting benefitted from the same. John always says in the class that apart from earning we should try to serve others it's the biggest virtue. Whatever little vision Ram has about a better life he can see that John is one person who could help him in achieving that.

Ram leaves the class and moves to Mahatma Gandhi (MG) road corner spot in the evening. Evening time is the peak time when the market is crowded. The corner just at the end of the initial entry pavement which runs parallel to one side of the road sees maximum crowd. Almost all the passerby crosses this point. It is a busy corner and a strategic location for boot polish persons. Ram sits here whenever he is on the MG road. Yes he has to share his earnings as an unofficial tax to the main person looking after this area. He settles down and opens his box and shouts in not so loud voice as "Boot Polish" "Boot Polish". He earns a little less than expected and winds up at night. "Mumbai trips are better money wise", he feels.

Next day again he goes to the railway station to catch the Pune-Mumbai train. Before that he buys a daily newspaper copy from one of the side hawkers. Today he came before time and manages to enter the general bogey of the train. After sitting on the entrance stairs for some time he moves inside saying loudly "Boot Polish", "Boot Polish". One person sitting on lower berth asks him "How much?" He says 2 Rs for one service. Person says ok. But before starting boot polish Ram hands over today's newspaper to him. He is little amazed at this as to why he is giving the newspaper. This is not a common sight or trend with boot polish walas[30] in India. Ram says that he daily buys a newspaper and offers the same to the client. This is a little free service he intends to provide his clients each day. The person is very much astonished at the answer. He could identify a spark in the child and so do I sitting at the other side in the same compartment. I am a journalist/writer and going to Mumbai for my work. I many a times travel by general compartment just to experience new people and their behaviors. I really liked his entrepreneurial skills at the first sight. This was a little unusual site for me that too in general compartment. After finishing the polish he moves on to the next person who is a foreigner. He looks like as if he was travelling for exploring the real India. "Would you like to get your boot polished", he asked in a fluent English accent. All other people around him are astonished at his fluent English speaking skills. Generally boot polish wala's are considered illiterate and acquiring fluent English accent is not at all their cup of tea. It is least expected from them. I was again taken aback by this kid. He continued with same thing of handing over the newspaper to this person who was by now familiar with the process. He finished up the work and went to the next compartment and I continued reading my current book. Just before reaching Mumbai I went to the washroom. After coming out I saw him again sitting on the stairs besides the gate. He was filling some details in a small notebook. I overlooked at his

---

[30] **Boot Polish Wala** is a person who is engaged in polishing boots. Walas in this context is a Hindi word most oftenly used for the person who polishes the shoe.

shoulder to see the page. He had a page where he was filling today's book keeping details:

Today's Earnings: ?
Today's Expenditure/Investment: ?
Today's Donation/Charity: ?
Daily Total: ?

I found him organized at his day to day dealings. It was a rare sight for me. He had filled all the section except "Donation" which was still empty. I asked him his name and about his family. What does he do apart from this? He told me that his name is "Ram" and said that he has an ailing mother in his family. He said he only does boot polish for living and also goes to one school for rest of the days. I really liked the kid and as train reached Dadar I left the train and moved out. Ram also left the train and found a place outside the station for boot polish. He worked there whole day just to pile up some of his savings.

He boarded another train in the evening returning to Pune. After reaching Pune he bought a wada pav (local maharashtrian burger) with some tea as an evening refreshment and donated one wada pav to a beggar. He completed his daily book keeping record at night filling up the all the details. He left the details in donation/charity section still empty. He never fills up the charity details but still keeps a section in his notebook just to remind himself for the same. He summed up all the details. This was his routine for those two days.

Next day also I saw him in the same compartment; he offered his newspaper and continued with his boot polish work. Person said, "I want a little more shine on my shoes". He rubbed the cloth again and moved on to the next person. Then as usual he got busy with another polishing. Just then a soft and gentle voice touched my ear doors.

It was a girl about nine years old. She was selling balloons. She was saying "Do you want balloons", 2 Rs each. She had only two heart shaped balloons left from her morning lot. Ram immediately stopped polishing and looked towards her. She also saw him and after a while he asked her to give one heart shaped balloon. He took that balloon and tied that in his knickers back side belt stripe. After finishing his work he moved to the same spot around the outer gate and as he reached there he saw her sitting there with her only remaining balloon. He asked her if he could sit there. She said ok. He sat just beside her and as I moved out of the compartment I saw both the heart shaped balloons touching each other from the back side. I found this sight a little romantic. Ram was updating his notebook for today's expenditure. I also left for my office and told about ram to one of my friends. He found this child a little unusual and he said that if he gets a good guidance and education then he can go places. It struck me at that point that let me give his name in the upcoming event for underprivileged children's. Top selected one will get a scholarship till 12ᵗʰ class. I enrolled his name and also told him about the event.

After that I did not see much of him and got engrossed in my usual work. I only got a chance to interact with him for those three days while travelling to my office in Mumbai. I was thinking of starting my own channel. After that I got busy researching about the same and left the country for better opportunity. To his good fortune, he was finally selected in that event and got the scholarship. I came to know about this through my friend later. I really felt good for him.".

This story flashed at my minds canvas after looking at that boot polish kid.

The young person sitting in front took out his old note book and started writing something in it. I overlooked him and saw that he is doing some book keeping work. I recognized the same pattern I have seen years back. I complimented him for this habit. And something just urged me to ask him "Are you Ram?"? He looked at me and then said with a feeling of astonishment "How do you know my name". I was relieved that I found him finally. I was worried about what happened to him. Though I had a little beard these days but he recognised me smilingly. And then we both exchanged the words about our past days. He is now an entrepreneur and thinking of starting his own channel. He became emotional while talking and said that he has been travelling in the general compartment of the same train for years hoping that one day he would meet the person who has changed his life. It is for this reason that he still keeps his old style of note book for book keeping hoping that one day he might see this and maybe he will recognize him. He held my hands and said "Thank You, Father". I could feel the wetness in my eyes. I somehow hold on to my tears.

My channel venture was successful abroad and now my team looks after it. I offered my help to him in his pursuit. We both left the compartment door talking to each other after train arrived at Dadar station, Mumbai. A girl also joined in later.

Another boot polish kid wearing a T-shirt with a neelkanth (The Indian Roller) bird print climbs up the stairs in the same general compartment with his wooden boot polish box shouting away "Boot Polish", "Boot Polish". Train leaves the station......

Be Happy
Bhavatu Sabba Mangalam

AN ENCOUNTER WITH TELEPATHY

———⊰※⊱———

It was September when he came to meet me. He was wearing a white dhoti[31] kurta[32] with a yellow robe around the neck. He was coming directly from Mathura, UP (India) to meet me. His name was Pandit Tulsi Ram. He was about fifty years of age. I did not have vehicle of my own at that time. I went to the Pune railway station along with my friend in his car to pick him up. We reached station just few minutes after train's arrival. After parking the vehicle I went inside the railway station. I tried his phone number and after some tries I got it through. He told me about his exact location but I could not locate him. As per my guess, I checked around the main station gate but could not find him there. Then I went to the other side of the station which has unreserved train ticket counters. There is a place just outside it where I could see many passengers coming out. I tried to look for him there and I could see him now after some effort; he was carrying a small hand bag standing at one side amongst the crowd. He saw me coming and smiled looking at me. I smiled back, picked up his hand bag and greeted him by touching his feet.

We left the railway station and took the route just beside the railway station. I asked him "How was the journey"? He smiled back and said it was ok. At that time I use to live in a rented row house. It took us about 30 minutes to reach the row house. After dropping us both; my friend went back to his home. I went upstairs and put his luggage in one of the bed rooms. We had two bedrooms on the first floor in that house. One of them was occupied by me and the other one was occupied by my office colleague named Prashant who also shared the apartment with me. He was currently out of station and had gone to his hometown. I took him upstairs till the room. I kept his luggage in the wardrobe and showed him the bath room. He took a shower bath and freshened up a bit. In the meantime I prepared the tea and arranged for some

---

[31] The **dhoti**, also known as veshti, mundu, pancha or mardani, is a traditional men's garment worn in the Indian subcontinent

[32] The term **kurta** is a generic term used in South Asia for several forms of upper garments for men and women, with regional variations of form.

snacks. I knocked his room door after sometime. He was just drying up his white dhoti after taking the bath. I went inside and offered him tea along with some snacks. We talked casually about few things over tea. I sensed that he was a bit tired after that long train journey. I thought that it would be good to have conversation in the evening. I asked him to take some rest. After that, I left home for some personal work. I came in evening and still remember I was sitting on the drawing room sofa when I saw him coming down through the staircase. The maid had prepared the dinner for two of us. She left in the evening after the work.

We did dinner together and I asked about his meditation place in Mathura.

"How is everybody at his home town"?

"How is his son doing"?

He replied "Everybody is fine and his meditation is progressing well". Meditation has become part of his daily routine now.

He was a resident of village koyla in Mathura district. He was a householder yogi. He has a meditation hut at river Yamuna passing nearby the village where he uses to meditate for long hours. He also has a get-together place for meditators and villagers just at the entry of the village. He has developed some small huts there as well for the regular mediators. But his long hours are mostly spent in his meditation hut by river Yamuna. Most of his intense samadhi states and spiritual research related work happened here. There are many popular anecdotes related to this place, which he shares once a while.

We started with the casual discussions about some spiritual topics but my main interest area that day was law of karma. I wanted to talk extensively about the law of karma and its manifestation in our lives. He said let us discuss it in detail the next morning. I got the chance next day after our breakfast. He was sitting on the sofa in drawing room and I was sitting on the floor just beside him when I asked him about some real life examples related to law of karma and how does it operate. To elaborate on it he told me about the story of 23 goats (which is a separate story in this book) and we discussed the different scenarios. Karma is always mutual and both parties carry that in their mind. Seeds of karma can only be burnt through intense meditation. I still remember one small analogy given by him for making me understand the cleansing process. He gave me an example of flock of wet sticks. If one wants to ignite the same it generally takes time but once ignited then even the other wet ones are also burnt. The ignition process is synonymous with daily meditation and the sticks resemble the karma seeds. He said forgiveness is the biggest tool we all have. If one forgives the other from heart then the other is also relieved of the mutual karma. While we were discussing this more, suddenly he stopped talking in between. I asked him if he is okay. Have I said something wrong? He replied the young girl has taken sleeping pills. It was out of context for me. We were discussing about law of karma and suddenly out of nowhere he spoke this sentence about some girl. He said that he needs to go to his room and need to meditate for some time. The discussion stopped in between. I also left for my company work. I met him in the evening time after the office. We again eat the dinner together and after that I asked him about that morning comment. He sat down on the sofa and told me the whole story. He said there is boy who works in his village meditation place at his home town. That boy also has a sister who used to sometimes visit the centre for cleaning purpose. She used to clean the place and looks after the place. In a way she does a "seva". He told me that he received a message in the morning that girl is not well and has taken too many sleeping pills and was admitted to a local hospital in emergency condition. Since he knows them personally and they take care of his place well. He has formed a heart connection with them. He generally gets a message if something goes wrong or they are in danger. It was a telepathic message that he received. This was my first encounter with telepathy. I asked him more about the same and then he told me that after leaving the sofa he went straight upstairs to his room and sat there in meditation for some time. He went to the hospital as out of the body experience and saw her there. She was slowly recovering now. The danger was over as a result of prompt action taken by the doctors. He said that there was a little dispute regarding her marriage. She was in a love relationship with a local village boy. She liked that boy much and wanted to spent rest of her life with him. Her family members did not agree to this due to some inter-caste issues. Though in metro cities the inter-caste marriages are accepted but these are still considered a taboo in the local village area in India. She was a pure hearted girl. So just out of helplessness and desperation she took too many sleeping pills. Doctors were also shocked at first. She is now recovering slowly. We had some other discussions and then I retired to my room and was thinking about the whole incident. I thought that I had observed telepathy today. It was how it worked. I was still unaware of the nitty gritties of it but had observed one. So the people who are connected with heart gets intuitive message about the others. Mother many a times gets intuitive message through dreams or telepathy about their children's, if something bad is about to happen or has happened. Telepathy is very common in mother child relationship.

This was my official first encounter with telepathy. That day is still young somewhere in my subconscious mind.

Be Happy
Bhavatu Sabba Mangalam

23 Goats

Kanha is at hospital bed since last 6 days. His father is very worried about his deteriorating health. Kanha was brought in the district government hospital when suddenly he had a severe migraine attack. He was getting seizures from past many days. His father consulted local doctor for his condition. Doctor gave some medications for the same and asked his father to take care of Kanha. Still after many days of medication his health was continuously degrading. He was now getting frequent migraine attacks. Local doctors advised his father to admit him immediately. It was when the situation got alarmingly bad his father admitted him to city district government hospital.

His father was a whole sale retailer in the city of Mathura (in state of UP, India). Kanha started to get these attacks just after when he was 2 years of his age. His father is taking care of him from that age. His first attack was very strange; he got unconscious after the attack and fell on the ground. His father took him instantly to the hospital. Doctors diagnosed him and gave him regular injections and glucose. Doctor told his father that mind fever could be the cause of falling unconscious. After this first attack; Kanha continued to get migraine attacks. Attack were sometimes that severe that his eyes used to roll over and his jaw was fixed where above and lower teeth's were tightly locked. He used to emit froth from his mouth with a hissing sound. The sight was horrifying for somebody else to see. Father also used to get terrified many a times at the sight. Being father he has to take care of his son. The frequencies of these attacks have increased in recent years. In previous years he used to get one or two such attack every year. Initially doctors gave medicine to just strengthen his conditions. But considering the current frequency they suggested some more medical tests based on which they suggested a 3 year course, where he was supposed to take medicines daily. The course was very rigorous in terms of execution as the only condition was that if medicines are missed a single day the counter will start from that day for another 3 years. It was a hard routine to follow but he did his best to continue it. He missed once where he had to again continue the medicine for another 3 years. Only condition with this medication is that the kid should be below 12 years of age. Kanha was 6 years of age as of now. Doctor suggested few more conditions that need to be taken care of along with this medication course. He is not allowed to see any Television programmes; he had to eat healthy food and had to take special precaution for sleeping early. Extra care and attention is required for Kanha which his father was giving at his best. Considering his condition and the degree of care that needs to be taken, he had even appointed one person for his retail shop. That person is now looking after the sales and father used to visit the shop once daily.

Life has become a little tough for father to manage after Kanha's mother expired last year. Father's younger sister decided to come to help his brother at this point. She knew that kanha would need a constant care at this time. A young child always needs mother attention and care more than his father. She was helping him and taking good care of Kanha now. It has hampered his studies also but everyone was hopeful that he would recover after this course. Father is also trying to spend more time at home now. After that last severe attack he has to remain at home to handle any emergency situation. Due to current circumstances father gradually had lost all interest in his retail shop business and the only thought occupying his mind was about kanha. Despite of this hard phase he was trying his level best to serve Kanha. Sometimes he use to sit alone and use to think about his son's worsening condition "what has he done to incur such hard life". The days passed and father with the help of his sister was able to complete the course as suggested by doctors. It was a daily task for 3 years which required continuity and patience. The thought of kanha's life again coming back to normalcy gave him enough strength to complete the course. His love for kanha was immeasurable. He took kanha for a final check up in the hospital. After some tests, doctors also gave a green signal that he should now be fine and migraine attacks should not happen again. Father also saw a drastic improvement in his condition after the course. Kanha was again back to life with vigour. He has also started playing with his old friends. After going through such tumultuous and challenging times his father also seem to be happy now and slowly regained his interest in his retail shop business. He became more active and was spending more time at the shop now.

One fine day kanha was playing outside the home and suddenly his friend called his aunt (father's sister) to come outside. She went outside in a hurry. Father was at his shop at that time. She saw Kanha was lying on the floor with his eyes rolling and locked jaw with froth and a hissing sound coming from his mouth. She was terrified at the sight and immediately sent somebody to call his father. Father immediately left the shop and ran towards his home. Father took him to hospital immediately where doctor's suggested to admit him without any delay. He could have got a severe migraine with brain fever.

Doctor's were not saying anything clear but father sensed that it could be something alarming from their level of attention.

In the meanwhile sister called up the elder sister who was married and was settled in a village named Koyla near Mathura. She knew about kanha's situation but this sounded a little severe and alarming to her as well. She took permission from her husband who was a psychic and a meditator and immediately left for the city hospital. She stayed there for couple of days and provided necessary support to kanha and his father. She also could not stand at the sight of this terrible condition of kanha and was really feeling sad for his brother. She was thinking the moment everything comes up to normal then again something new comes up. After the course was completed she was also relieved and was positive about kanha's recovery. She left hospital after 2 days. She was really worried about kanha and consulted her husband in this regard. She asked him if he could do something about this. Is there any way of knowing, what is causing such pain and misery to her brother. He consoles her and says that he will see whatever best he can do from his side. He said that he will meditate and will try to look for the possible cause of it. She persuaded him to visit the hospital once to see kanha's worsening condition. On her insistence he agreed to visit hospital. He was generally a meditator and use to meditate for long hours alongside river Yamuna. He had a small hut along the river where he used to spent long hours in meditation sometimes the whole night. He rarely visits anybody and people often come to his house for consultation. His wife takes care of all the household chores and she also takes care of him selflessly.

Next day they both went to hospital to see kanha. She entered first followed by her psychic husband. As he entered the room and made eye contact with kanha lying on a corner bed, kanha also looked in his eyes as if he is replying back and smiled towards him. Nobody could grasp what has happened except the meditator. His wife was curious to know and asked him was he able to trace the problem. He kept quiet and sat for some time near kanha's bedside. He put his hand on his head as if he is blessing him. After that, he met his brother-in-law and they discussed about his current condition. Then they both left the hospital in the evening time. On the way to Mathura his wife asked him what is the matter with kanha.

"Were you able to sense something?" she asked him again.

She also asked "Why did he smile back at you"?

He avoided the question as if he wants to ignore something.

But she asked again.

After much insistence he told his wife. Do you really want to know? She said yes. Then he narrated in his equivocal voice that "Kanha will expire day after tomorrow at the noon time". He was not at all emotional while saying this. She was taken a back at the revelation. And he continued, before that his father will pay the bills last time. She could not grasp this and felt as if something has hit her mind. She was already worried about kanha and her brother. And now this revelation came as a shock to her. She remained silent for some time looking straight in her husband's eyes as if she is not happy about this. After a deep silence she still managed to ask the reason for it. She did not want to believe this and then he narrated the back story:

"In one of the past birth kanha was a simple goat herder and he used to love his goats very much. He used to visit different villages for feeding his goats. They use to eat roadside green vegetation. In summers the weather gets really hot in Mathura and the road side vegetation is also scarce and most of the time gets burnt. No matter how harsh is the weather he has always looked after his goats and was able to find landscapes with vegetation sometimes in other villages. He had a herd of 23 goats. He was an orphan and his whole world revolves around his goats. Taking care of them was his only work and he use to do that religiously.

One summer there was a severe draught and there was no vegetation left for goats. All the roadside vegetation was burnt in scorching heat. Also the crop fields were dried up. It was an alarming and tough time for kanha. He had to sustain his goat herd. His primary goal was to give them something to eat. As he was passing by a local shop, the shop owner asked him about the goats. He said they have grown weak due to insufficient green vegetation. He suggested him to go to landlords shop. He will surely help him. He could not see any other way out and immediately went to the shop along with his goats. Landlord has seen his herd flock many a times while he use to pass by his shop. He had plenty of husk and green chopped vegetation which he was now selling to villagers. As this was draught time it was selling very well with a rate higher than usual. Kanha asked him for some vegetation which he refused immediately. He said he could give the vegetation only after he agrees to put his goat herd as security. He said that he had to give his thumb impression on an agreement for this. Kanha didn't know much about this and had no option but to agree for the same. His only primary concern was to feed his goats. Landlord agreed to give him fresh fodder for few months. Goats were better now after the feed. These were hard times for everybody. Kanha went again after few days to have next slot of vegetation husk. Landlord refused him the promised lot this time. Kanha pleaded but he disagreed. He said that he own the goats now as kanha has sold all his flock to him. Kanha got furious at this. By this time landlord men have already got hold of the flock. He said this is cheating he should return his goats. Landlord asks his men to throw kanha out of the village and captured all his goats. Kanha loved his goats so much that he could not recover from this shock. He grew thin and stopped eating any food. He could not take the thought of his goats out of his mind and was just thinking continuously about them. All his life he has served his goats and he had no other being to talk too. He could not take this shock and ultimately starved to death after few days.

She asked what happened after that. How is the story related to our kanha. He again continued the narration and said: "That boy kanha is our Kanha in current birth while that landlord has taken birth as his father. His father has to pay all the karmic debt back to kanha. He is doing that for many years and last installment will be paid day after tomorrow. After that Kanha will leave his body peacefully. His father will pay the final bill to the doctor before his departure. She could not believe this but he said such are karmic debts we all are bound by laws of nature. She asked then "Why did he smiled at you?" He replied that kanha himself is aware of this fact and he could see that I also know this fact now. He could sense that I have seen his past birth after that first eye contact with him. He smiled that finally he will be relieved from this debt. Strange was this but she could only wait for the outcome. They both left day after tomorrow to the hospital. In the afternoon at about 1:30 pm he again got a severe migraine attack, his father had gone to pay the bills. Kanha smiled one last time towards the psychic who blessed him to have a good after life. Just as kanha's father returned back after paying the bills he saw kanha is no more.

She still hasn't revealed the kanha's past birth story to her brother and holds this in her heart. She has now started to believe her husband and started taking active interest in this spiritual/karmic law.

Be Happy
Bhavatu Sabba Mangalam

SEVEN AND HALF
(STORY OF A KARMA CLEANSING)

It was Friday when I took half day off from the office and left for Mumbai. My younger brother was working in an electronic giant TV maker company. He was working there as a research assistant trying to figure out new features for the TV remote. He was busy in his work when I called him up that I would be reaching there by evening time. He was staying there in one of Andheri East, Mumbai residential buildings. He was sharing apartment with one of his friends.

I planned to leave for Mumbai from Pune bus stand. Bus stand was just beside the railway station. While going to bus stand we have to cross the railway station. I reached railway station by an autorickshaw. I did not have a vehicle of my own in those days. After reaching station I started to walk towards the bus stand when in between I was stopped by a young person, who suggested hiring a shared cab. I said, "I will go by bus". He insisted that taking a seat in the shared cab would be a comfortable and a cheaper option. I thought for a while and said ok, let's try that. He was a travel agent and took me to the nearby cab. Cab was almost full with just one seat left at the back side. I boarded the cab and we left for Mumbai. While sitting at the back side, I was looking outside through the front window. I do not know why but my eyes were always getting fixed on the small "Sai Baba" idol firmly attached at the centre of the cab's dashboard.

All through my journey till I reached Mumbai, I experienced this behavior quite often when my eyes got fixed on that "Sai Baba" idol. I reached Mumbai and hired an autorickshaw[33] till my brother's place. I spent about two days there and we had a good time together. We had many discussions ranging from the general to spiritual topics. We went to a multiplex to watch a movie and enjoyed the evening. It was after two days on Monday morning that I left his apartment back to Pune. I reached at Andheri east local train

---

[33] **Autorickshaw** are a common means of public transportation in many countries in the world. An autorickshaw is a usually three-wheeled cabin cycle for private use and as a vehicle for hire.

station and bought a train ticket. The ticket line was so over-crowded that it took some time to reach at the ticket window. After buying the ticket, I went inside on the concerned platform and waited for the arrival of next local train to Dadar[34]. The local train frequency in Mumbai is very good. We do not have to wait for too long. I saw the train approaching and boarded the train till Dadar. Local trains on weekday mornings are very crowded especially on the popular routes. Somehow I also got into one of the second class bogey. It was so crowded that I was just using my one foot to sustain the weight of my upper body in that crowd. People were rushing in and rushing out at the in-between stations. Everything seems to be at a rhythmic pace and the whole activity of getting inside and getting-out took no more than few seconds. It was such a tussle to get inside the bogey. Local people seem to have mastered this style. Only I was a new comer to this environment. Dadar stop was approaching and I somehow managed to get out at the station. I came outside from railway station and walked towards the local bus stand. I planned to take a bus back to Pune. It was not an official stand but there were many travel agent shops just under one of the outside over bridge. I crossed the over bridge and took right turn to reach at one of the shops. I asked him "When is the next bus to Pune"? He said in about "Half an hour". I asked, "How much is the ticket? He said "Rs 220". I argued with him that it's not reasonable. I told him that "I came from Pune in Rs 180". After some arguments he agreed with my bargain. He asked me to hand over the cash to book the ticket. As I tried to put my hand in the right back pocket, I was surprised to find that my wallet was not there. I was shocked as it contained all my cards and cash. I checked it again in left side and the front pockets but it was nowhere to be found. He waited for me and then I said do not book it now. He looked at me in surprise and almost stared at me saying that "If you do not have the money then what's the point of argument". I told him that my wallet got lost. I was in a state of fix. I did not know where to find it. I stood there for some time thinking what to do now. I was recalling what could have happened. I retraced the same way till Dadar station just looking on the road for my wallet. I tried this two three times but could not find it. At the end I just stopped under one big neem[35] tree

---

[34] **Dadar** is a neighborhood in Mumbai(India), and is also a railway station on both the Western (Dadar) and Central lines (Dadar T.T.) of the Mumbai Suburban Railway network.

[35] **Neem** (*Azadirachta indica*) is a tree in the mahogany family Meliaceae. It is native to India, Myanmar, Bangladesh, Sri Lanka, Malaysia and Pakistan. It grows in tropical and semi-tropical regions.

at the corner turn. I was not happy with this situation and was feeling bad as all my cash and cards (ATM, PAN Card etc) were there in wallet. Then while thinking for my next move as I turned towards my right I saw a very big "Sai Baba" picture frame just under that tree. In a state of restlessness, I literally cursed him for doing that bad to me. I remembered the whole journey while coming to Mumbai Sai Baba idol was getting highlighted again and again. And here it was once again under the tree. I came to senses after a while and called my brother. I told him about the incident. He said he might have the card details with him which probably I had shared with him some times back. He found them and called the bank for blocking it then and there as our first damage control step. He told me that credit card has been blocked. I also had an ATM card which was safe as it required a Personal Identification Number(PIN) which was not easy to guess. I again started to think where it could have happened.

I remembered there was a strong back push at one of the in-between stations. I was not sure but probably it happened there. After a while my brother called me up and informed me that he would be reaching Dadar station in some time. He took half day off from his office. I waited there for him and after he arrived we both consulted one traffic police person about this incident. He suggested to lodge an FIR at Dadar railway police station. It also appeared to us as our next step in this Sherlock Holmes journey. We now proceeded towards the Dadar station and reached platform number one via an internal platform over bridge. Dadar station is a big junction and has many platforms ranging from the central line to western line. As we came downstairs from the over bridge, we inquired about the railway police station. Someone guided us towards the station. It was at one end of the long platform stretch. The commuters generally occupy the centre part of the platform. This end had many people standing there with their big plastic cargo luggage. We made our way towards the railway police station door. The platform clock was hanging just above us as if watching our each and every activity with time. We could only stare at it now just to check the day time.

At the same time I was trying to block my ATM card through the bank's customer care service. As we entered the police station, the sub inspector there asked us to sit down and state our problem. We narrated the whole incident to him. He asked us to write all the factual details about the sequence of events along with attaching the Photostats of tickets if possible. My brother stayed there and I went to take photostat of tickets from outside the station. After taking photostat as I was approaching the station I got a message on my mobile saying that "You have bought Jewelry from K jewelers worth 400". I was shocked to see this as we have already blocked the card about an hour back. So how could it be possible that somebody used the credit card for the purchase? Then I thought that it's only Rs 400 which was not a big amount. I could not believe somebody buying such a cheap item. I read the message again which had several lines. As I read the previous line I saw it was "Rs 25". Ohh I got it then, somebody bought the Jewelry of Rs 25,400. Now I was taken aback. It was a blow and shock at the same time as the card was blocked hours back. I stayed there for some time and then went inside the station along with the Photostat. Police man asked the time of the theft. I said "I do not know". So we entered an approximate time as per the starting time mentioned on the ticket. I showed the message to my brother and we thought "How is it possible" as the card was already blocked. We guessed that the transaction must have been just before the card block. The thief was very clever and he did not wasted any minute in the golden opportunity he had in his lap. We shared the message with sub inspector and completed the FIR at Dadar station with full details. We took the duplicates of the FIR copy for our reference. The police sub inspector asked us to visit Andheri East railway police station once as the address of the jeweler comes under that area. We had no option but to pursue this till end. We felt determined to dig it further and left Dadar for Andheri east railway police station. On reaching there we told the inspector about the event. He showed us the old criminal record file containing the black and white photos of the convicts. He wanted us to identify the person amongst them. We tried to explain him that we even did not know who it was or when it was done. It was just approximate time that we are aware of. So we decided it was useless to spent time there. We thought we will investigate this by ourselves. We tightened our belts for the future adventures. By now we could get a little glimpse of how it feels to be in shoes of Mr. Sherlock Holmes. But we were excited to pursue this one. Our first destination was K Jewelers. Sun has already set and it was evening time of a long and an event full day. We took a break at Mac Donald's Burger counter as if we are charging our batteries for coming events and ordered two vegetable burgers. I was feeling a bit relaxed in my mind even after such an unexpected ordeal that we went through in the day. I was feeling that whatever will happen; will happen for our good. After that we moved on towards the K jewelers shop after a local inquiry about the address. We got some idea but needed to find it on our own. After some hit and trial we finally saw a big board over the shop with "K Jewelers" written on it. Yes this was it. We walked inside and reached at their reception counter. The sales person came forward and attended us. We told him about the credit card theft that took place this afternoon. The sales person became fearful on hearing "credit card theft" and kept silent. He did not spoke for some time and then called the shop owner. He came from inside and asked us "What is the matter"? We told him that a credit card was swiped this afternoon for buying a gold chain. He said yes there was gold chain sale transaction this afternoon. We said it was a fraud transaction and asked him further "Do you remember the person?" He was taken aback for some time and thought we are from CID (Crime Investigation Department) which he disclosed later to us. He told us that "Yes he remembers that person". We asked him "Did you check the Identity card of that person"? He said it was our first customer of the day (first customer is of importance in Indian culture) and they forgot to check the details. As per the norms it is mandatory to see the identity card details before any jewelry sale. Had they done that, he would have been caught then and there. Then sales person came forward and told us that he is now getting to understand "Why he has used that Yellow tape at the back side of the card. He probably wanted to hide the original signature". We asked him further about the yellow tape. He then told us that he inquired about the signature at the back side of the card which was done over a yellow tape. He asked the customer that "Why has he used the yellow tape at the signature area?" Customer replied that the portion got corrupted so he put a tape and has signed over it. Sales person frowned a bit on hearing this, as it was a little strange behavior to have the signature like this. He told us that he still remembers the signature name, it was "D Kumar". We could now guess that he had used the yellow tape to hide the original one and to show the forged signature. Credit card pin was not mandatory at that time so the chances for fraud were a possibility. So most of the shopkeeper used to check the signature at the back side of the card and use to tally it with the front side card holder's name. This was the basic check many of the shop keepers use to follow. The execution of fraud was pretty clear to us now. We now were looking for some concrete evidences to nab him. The shop owner showed us the duplicate copy of the bill and gave us one Photostat version for our reference. Sales person further added that he was wearing earring in his right ear and had French cut beard. He was around 35-40 years of age. By now we got the photostat copy of the bill and some information. We exchanged their phone numbers and thanked them for the cooperation. The next move was the nearest police station. Sherlock looked towards Holmes and Holmes looked back as if a decision happened in their eyes for the next move. We were about to leave just then one of shop attendant came forward and informed us that they could also see that fraudster. It was a sudden turn of events. We asked with a fresh tone "How"? He told us that they keep the CCTV[36] video footage of last 7 days. Sherlock and Holmes were charged again as our investigation has taken a new turn. "Please take us there" was our reply. Few seconds later we were in their control room where he showed us the actual footage of that person buying the gold chain. We thought it is good evidence and he was clearly visible from a distance. We got something concrete now and planned to take a break that day. We decided to move to Police station the next morning as we have now got enough information to nab him. After such a hectic and chaotic day and despite of being darkness outside we sensed some light inside. The excitement of unearthing the truth was enough to make us move on to the next day. Sherlock (myself) and Holmes (my brother) bid farewell to the day and returned to Holmes residence and thought about the strategy for next day. Holmes went to office in first half and took off for second half.

At that time I use to work for a software company working on the ATM[37] kiosks software for the US market. So my knowledge of the ATM domain was pretty well. I thought of calling the credit card bank customer care again. I called them up and narrated the whole incident. I asked them about the information regarding card usage history which he refused to divulge at first. After some persuasion from my side he told me about the usage history. He told me that the first transaction done was of Rs. 25400 at K Jewelers which I was aware of. Then he told me about several other declined transaction at different jewelers. He was just going for a big hit but due to our quick action on blocking the card we were saved of these transactions. He also told me that the person tried to take out the money from ATM but it was declined due to incorrect PIN. ATM machine allows cash out on credit cards but only after the correct pin. He tried at several ATM's in that area. I insisted him on giving the ATM Id's and the time of the transaction (the term I was aware as I worked in ATM domain. Each ATM machine has a unique ID). He refused at first but gave the information after explaining the situation I was in. He also helped me with useful information that each ATM kiosk has a camera so

---

[36]   Closed-circuit television (**CCTV**), also known as video surveillance, is the use of video cameras to transmit a signal to a specific place, on a limited set of monitors.

[37]   An **automated teller machine** or automatic teller machine (**ATM**), also known as an automated banking machine (ABM, Canadian English), cash machine, cashpoint, cashline, or colloquially hole in the wall (British and South African English), is an electronic telecommunications device that enables the customers of a financial institution to perform financial transactions without the need for a human cashier, clerk or bank teller.

his snap should have been captured in those ATM's. By now I was confirmed that our case is building up well with some concrete evidences. I thanked the customer care guy from the bottom of my heart. By that time my brother also came in home and I shared this information with him. We discussed about the next step and thought of going to the media for this case. Then we thought that let us first go to the main police station of that area.

As we stepped out of our apartment we wore the shoes of Sherlock and Holmes again. Sherlock and Holmes got ready with all the latest information and went to the main police station. After some time we got a chance to have a word with the constable. He immediately denied and said we should go to the jeweler area police station. He did not even listen to our story. Holmes got irritated with him and exchanged some harsh word with the person. Sherlock felt like as if everybody was just playing a ping pong ball with them. After that we left main station in search of the jeweler's area police station with a heavy mind. We reached the station after about half an hour. We inquired about the station in charge. A constable took us to the inspector in charge. Inspector was very cooperative person and very patiently listened to our story. He seems to be a well-educated person. He was communicating to us in English. This was a rare sight for Sherlock in India. We told him about all the evidences and proofs. We were excited that we would be able to nab him now. After listening to us the next thing he spoke was a little shocking for both of us. He told us that we do not have the right to file a case for credit card theft. We were amazed after hearing this piece of information. He told us that only the issuer bank has the right to file the FIR(First Information Report) for investigation. This investigation has to be channeled through the bank. We still insisted him about all the hard work of evidence collection that we did in two days. He said that's fine and asked us to submit an application attaching photostats of all proof including railway ticket, jewelry bill and ATM ID records for the transactions. Sherlock wrote a quick application and went outside to take all Photostats again. He stapled them with the application and submitted in the station. Station in charge suggested us that we should file a complaint about card theft in the bank and then they will initiate the investigation process from there end. It would certainly not be a day's job and might take many days. He told us that banks generally have cards insured so in such cases if fraud is declared then banks will claim their money. The spirit of Sherlock and Holmes was dying and we thought a little defeated as all the evidences are in front of us and we just need to take action. We thought if we could recover his snap from the corresponding ATM then we can even show that on local channel and the culprit would be caught in days. But after listening to the station in charge we thought that everybody is protected and in such case the thief might go un-nabbed. Sherlock was not happy with this information. But we left the station thanking him for all the cooperation. We reached the bank head quarter branch by evening time and filed a complaint about the lost card. They told us that new card will be issued and will reach Sherlock's address within next week. Also they will check the transaction and if declared fraud it will be shown as negative amount in Sherlock's next credit card bill. So for now it is charged but by next bill in case fraud is proved it will be shown as negative amount and Sherlock will not have to pay this amount. Sherlock was a little relieved at this but also had a feeling whether the main culprit will be caught or not. We wanted him to be caught at any cost. This moment appeared to be the end of our Sherlock Holmes journey. We really felt like detectives working on uncovering the truth. We came to our normal selves after this moment. Last two days were busy but exciting. As a double check I submitted all the evidence details with the corresponding Photostats in the bank headquarter as well. It was an end of two days of detective work but we were not fully happy as the person who could have been caught immediately still has a chance to escape. All now depends on the result of investigation.

We came home and I left for Pune the next day. I was a little extra cautious this time while travelling the local train from Andheri to Dadar. I had to take two days leave from office after this incident. I thought that the whole incident left a bad taste in my mouth. It was still not over as I will have to wait for next month's credit card bill about the final resolution. As I reached Pune and left the station for my rented apartment I took a walk initially to catch the bus from next stop. As I was approaching the bus stand I saw a fakir with two of his pupil holding on the green cloth sheet for collecting the alms. They came all of a sudden in front of me and prompted me for alms. As I looked up towards the fakir, I saw that fakir is holding a small Sai Baba's photo in his hands. Suddenly, I felt that Sai Baba's photo/idol which has been following my mind all through my journey is right again in front of me. I felt like donating all the money I had with me and did so. My eyes got wet as I was feeling that Sai Baba has taken all my wealth. I also felt like a fakir at that point of time. Fakir came up to me and blessed me. I left then with a heavy heart looking towards the sky. I was feeling that god has once again bereft me of all my wealth. I walked down towards the bus stop with a heavy heart and stood there waiting for the next bus. I reached my home with some last penny I found in some corner of my wallet.

After few days, a person came looking for me. He rang the apartment bell and as I opened the door he told me that he is the investigating officer from banks side. I invited him in and he told me that he will close this investigation. I showed him all the evidence and shared all the concerned photostats with him. He left after some time ensuring that it will be declared as fraud.

At the start of next month I got the monthly statement where the transaction for Rs 25400 was shown as negative and fraud was written against that transaction. The case was finally closed after all that mental agony. I discussed this case with my father's guru who used to do meditation at the banks of river Yamuna in a village near Mathura (U.P). He said to me after analyzing my horoscope that I have just passed "Sadhe Saati – i.e. Seven and Half". He told me that there are three such phases in everybody life span and mine was second. He said that you are blessed that there is no physical harm done otherwise most people face many such incidents as accidents, physical damage, loss of money etc. He said that you incurred only the monetary loss and that too is recovered. So you just had a mental agony and have come out from that safe. Immediately then I realized the significance of that "Sai Baba" getting visible in all those forms, the idol, the picture under tree and the last at that fakir outside the railway station. I then realized that in reality he protected me all through my journey and that day I stopped cursing him. I thanked him from the bottom of my heart. The incident is still alive and we share that once a while.

Be Happy
Bhavatu Sabba Mangalam

Michael and Goldwin: The two Neighbors

A parcel is on the way to one of the bungalows in Beverly Hills. The post man arrives and moves towards one of the bungalows. He looks at the name plate which is being renovated and takes a pause. He could see "Bridges" written on it and the other parts are under renovation. He verifies the same on the parcel. He checks for the letter box and could not find one. He then looks at the renovation work going on inside and moves towards the bungalow gate. He rings the bell and after some time a maid comes from inside in a state of hurry as if something has occupied her mind. She was busy inside looking after and coordinating the renovation work. She receives the parcel quickly and moves inside. The work was in its completion stages and will take another day or two.

Michael is having his morning coffee and is trying hard to relax. He does not seem to be in a relaxed state of mind at all. He is looking at some papers and is bit worried and tense about something. He sips his black coffee again and looks at the papers with a little tense look. Something is bogging his mind down.

The maid comes in between having a parcel in the hand and hands it over to Michael. Michael is so engrossed in the papers that he asks her in a bit harsh tone, "Do not disturb me; put it in my bedroom". She knew the master is a bit worried these days, she accepts the harsh tone as part of her duty. She goes on the first floor and puts the parcel besides the bed on the side table.

Michael had a successful dairy brand which he established all by himself. He toiled hard to set up his business. He has provided employment to number of people. But everyone knew that he is an arrogant business man and sometimes takes very harsh decision if required. He has taken many cost cutting measures at the workplace. His brand had an outward appeal due to his initial work but not everyone was happy with him these days. He had cut throat competition in the market which along with his arrogant attitude is affecting the sales. Productivity took a down turn for him this season. As a result, he has incurred huge debts this season. His business is on the brink of closing down. His house maid has also realized his excessive arrogant behavior. However, she has adapted herself and does her duty well. Somewhere she had realized that this is more so due to his current business crisis and issues.

After keeping the parcel the maid again bothers him by asking, "Sir please check the list of guests invited two days later for the party at home". Michael gives a stubborn and arrogant look. Michael has a TO DO list which he has handed over to his maid and asked her to remind him about the same. She has seen the item in his TO DO list and she is looking after all the preparation at home for his upcoming birthday party coordinating with Michael's personal manager who is the overall in charge.

A slight renovation is happening on the front gate around the name plate area. "It should be finished by today day end" she thinks optimistically. She gets busy in coordinating all other work.

Goldwin is busy in the morning Vipassana meditation session at his residence. He lives in a bungalow adjacent to Michael's bungalow. People know him well in this neighborhood and he is popular for conducting morning one hour meditation sessions regularly. As usual he has got quite a good gathering from this Beverly Hills neighborhood. He has just completed one hour session and is now doing Mangal Maître (Thanks giving meditation - Sharing our merits with others).

Goldwin is a stained glass artist and sculptor. He is very humble and good natured person. Everybody knows him in the vicinity and calls him "The Meditation Man". Most people like his hospitality and generous nature and attend his morning meditation sessions. He has just completed the daily morning session and is heading up for the coming day's work.

He is busy in building a sculptor these days. He has just started it and it will take some more days looking at his current speed. He is making it with Plaster of Paris. He enjoys his work very much.

Michael is gearing up for the meetings scheduled this morning. As he has incurred many losses in the dairy business so he is constantly thinking of reviving his business with a fresh new approach. He does not want to lose the advantage and name he has garnered over years in dairy industry. He is thinking of a new approach, a new strategy perhaps for making a name again. He is busy reviewing many new ideas but is not getting the right one. This year has been a year of losses. Back at home, his maid is taking care of all the arrangements for the upcoming birthday party. The arrangement this year is a low affair and does not match the arrangement and grandeur of the last year party.

For birthday party Michael asked his personal manager to look after the invitees. The party started with all the pomp and fare. Some people who are also the mutual friend of Goldwin inquired about his absence. They were expecting Goldwin also as he is an immediate neighbor of Michael. But he was nowhere to be seen. Michael was avoiding questions about Goldwin that evening. Those inquiries about Goldwin's presence reminded him about the altercation he had with Goldwin sometimes back. Goldwin was trying to suggest few things to him in a common get-together some months back which Michael disliked and it turned out to be a spat. Goldwin was aware of the business issues he was going through and wanted to help Michael. Michael took it personal and became arrogant. The party went on and finished very late night.

Next morning Michael woke up a little late and as he went by living area he could see many gifts lying there. He came back and looks at the parcel lying on his bedside table and opens the outer wrapper. He finds a strange bronze antique bowl with a padded mallet made of wood. He could not figure that out and thought that perhaps it was a birthday gift. He took the outer wrapper and put it in the bed side table drawer just to clear the space over the table. His mind is most of the time occupied with his office and business issues. He was about to explore more, immediately he got a call. He left the room and went to the balcony and got indulged in the conversation.

Michael's Tibetan maid brought his morning coffee and as she turned back after keeping the tray on one of the bed side tables, the bowl kept on the other side table caught her attention. She recognized it immediately and some old memories passed by her mind. She walked across the bed toward the table and picked up the bowl and padded wooden mallet. She just sat there and could not resist herself playing it. A very soothing first harmonic started to emanate from it and the room was filled with its harmonic voice.

Michael overheard it while still on the call. He heard it for the first time and felt it soothing to ears. He found the voice overpowering and it stopped after a while. The maid saw that Michael has noticed her, so she put it back and returned to kitchen area.

After finishing the call, Michael asked his maid that where the sound was coming from. She was apprehensive in the start and then explained it to Michael that she played the singing bowl kept at your bedside table.

Michael: "Is it for playing?" I could not figure it out.
Maid: Yes it for playing; we used to play when I was in Tibet. I learned
          it there. It is a popular meditation technique in Tibet. They have

named it "Singing Bowl Meditation". Some people also call it as "Himalayan Bowl".

Michael: Can you bring it here and play in front of me?

Maid: Sure sir.

She brought the bowl and played in front of the master.

Michael was really pleased to hear that one. He decided to hear it daily before going out.

Michael: Would you teach me how to play it?

Maid: Sure sir. It will be my pleasure.

He learned to play it from her and started to play daily during morning hours.

During morning sessions he saw Goldwin in his balcony enjoying the first harmonic sound. His facial expression with closed eyes suggested as if he is enjoying the vibration and finding it soothing to his ears. Both their balconies were adjacent to each other. Michael ignored him initially but he was aware that Goldwin also has started to come in his balcony daily during his morning singing bowl session. He noticed him but did not have a conversation.

This new routine has a positive effect on Michael's nature. He has finally started to learn the art of relaxation and by nature became less arrogant. This was turning out to be a positive change as far as his business is concerned. His dairy business again started to show positive sales growth after a change in the brand name. With the different brand name he managed to stick the right chord with customers. People at his work place also noticed this change in Michael's behavior. They were happy about it. He made a basic change in strategy to launch his new product. After some research, he chooses to have glass bottle instead of plastic one in order to differentiate the products. This new change though well researched but still was a market gamble for him, may be the last one. After the launch on some test outlets, this gamble of his soon began to become a hit among the youth customers. With this initial market acceptance, he decided to provide many flavored milk options. He got the market niche as other competitors were not providing these flavors.

Deep in his subconscious mind he started to feel a sense of attachment to that singing bowl. It almost became as a good omen for him.

One fine day as he was finished up with the morning bowl session, a thought came to his mind. He considered this gift as a special one. He became curious and just wanted to know who has gifted such a life changing gift. He felt a strong feeling of gratitude towards the person for this valuable gift. He tried to remember about the gift wrapper as he could recall that he had kept it somewhere. After a while, he remembered where he had kept that wrapper. He went straight up to his side table drawer and tried to look out for that wrapper. It was beneath some other documents and after searching for some time he was able to find it.

The next morning he went out his gate and went straight towards Goldwin's bungalow gate. He saw people coming out of Goldwin's bungalow after completing morning group meditation session. As he reached near the gate, he saw Goldwin and waved his hand as if he is calling him.

Goldwin saw him and came out. He asked him "what's the matter now"? Is everything ok?

Michael: "I wanted to return you something"
Goldwin: "Return"... What is that?

Michael handed over the packet of Singing Bowl to Goldwin.

At this Goldwin asked "What is it and why are you giving it to me?"

Michael said this is your parcel containing a singing bowl and by mistake it has been delivered at his bungalow. At this Goldwin remembered that once he has ordered this online but he did not track it later and was thinking of ordering another one.

Then Michael told him the whole story: When he checked the old packet wrapper in his drawer and finds to his amazement that the parcel's actual recipient was Goldwin Bridges and not Michael Bridges, he was puzzled how it has arrived at his bungalow. The parcel had arrived from Tibet. In the hurry of Birthday rush and gifts he mistook it for his own gift. Actually, it was due to his renovation work where the post man could only see "Bridges" on the nameplate. The first name and the other details were under repair. The letter box was also under repair. The postman did not check twice and mistook it for Goldwin Bridges bungalow and delivered it at his bungalow.

Goldwin could sense the change in his behavior while he narrated the incidents. He felt little surprised after seeing this humble behavior from Michael. He was not expecting this after that last spat. He even thought for a while whether he was talking to that old Michael or a completely new one. He could figure out that he is a changed person now, a much calmer and peaceful.

Michael handed over the packet and insisted Goldwin "Please take your stuff back?"

On seeing such a friendly behavior Goldwin thought, this thing has brought such a nice change in Michael's behavior. He also remembered those morning sessions as he himself was the part of them. He personally liked the change and was happy about it. He said to Michael, "Please keep this with you". He had never taken the altercation happened with him on his heart. Please consider it as a small Birthday gift from his side.

At first Michael hesitated and felt a little embarrassed as he had not even invited him on his recent Birthday bash. Michael asked him again to take it back. But Goldwin smiled at him and insisted on keeping it with him. Please accept it as a token of our new friendship.

Michael smiled and both shook hands and became friends again.

Now many a times they both enjoy the Singing bowl together. Michael also has learned about Vipassana meditation from Goldwin. He has also attended one 10 day basic course and now attends morning sessions in Goldwin bungalow. Michael also has started the morning Vipassana meditation session in his bungalow. Some days the session is held at Goldwin's bungalow and someday at Michael's bungalow. Both have become much happier person.

Michael has also started to take sculpting lessons from Goldwin.

Goldwin is busy finishing up his latest sculpting piece. He is finishing up the sculptor of Shri S.N. Goenka Ji, a Burmese-Indian teacher of Vipassana meditation. He is hoping to complete it soon.

Be Happy
Bhavatu Sabba Mangalam

Reiki Session

——◆——

After having a detailed conversation with "The Water Yogi" I moved out of his room. As I was slowly walking in the corridor towards my room I happened to see commandant sitting and discussing something with another person in a double occupancy adjacent room. The BSF (Border Security Force) commandant and the other person; who was his roommate were sitting on their respective cots and were having a conversation when I entered in their room. BSF commandant knew me as we had an unfinished mantra story discussion sometimes back in Water yogi's room. I sat alongside his roommate and became a silent listener for some time. I was really curious to know the end and wanted to know more about that mantra story.

I did not interrupt their conversation and listened patiently to them. Then as their discussion got finished I asked the commandant about that mantra story. He gave a little brief about the starting part of the story for other person to pick up the context. And when everybody was on the same page he narrated the remaining part.

"Then after few days he got a casual knife wound while peeling off the fruits at his juice shop. He thought of using the same mantra and recited it, as to his astonishment the wound healed immediately. He could not believe his eyes as things like this were a fairytale for him. Many days passed and he now has begun to help his father at the juice shop occasionally. He did not share this mantra with anybody and has kept the mantra hidden only in depths of his heart. He got busy with his daily routine and after many days once again the opportunity came where he was faced with one such incident when he was taking bath under a common water tap. As he stood up, the water tap pierced at the centre of his head and blood started coming out profusely from the wound. He recited the same mantra and the head skin got fixed immediately and the wound healed instantaneously. This was again a miraculous effect for child like him. After this incident he sometimes started to reveal it to others and started talking openly about it. People used to laugh about it and some of his friends would look at his face in amazement and could not believe him. And then the same happened which the yogi had already warned for, one fine day when he wanted to use the mantra, he was unable to recall it. He tried hard to recall the mantra but it was erased from his subconscious mind. Despite of his several attempts he could not recall even some part of it. He had completely forgotten that mantra now. It stayed with him and served him for about two years. May be because he was revealing it to others or the life of the mantra with him was over. Whatever might be the reason but the truth is that he forgot that mantra after which he was not able to use it again anymore. This was his little short story. The mantra was gone but the memory of that story remained with him till this date. During our further discussion he told us that he is now a retired person and planning to start his own hotel near Dehradun. He was a local resident of Dehradun. As he was speaking to us he felt a little back pain at the lower side of his spinal cord and he lied down on his cot. We got concerned and the other person curiously asked him "What is the matter?" Commandant replied that nothing, he is suffering from a chronic back pain. He told us that he has been living with this pain for about last nine years now. He has now left all hopes of getting rid of this one. It has become a part of his daily routine and he has even learned to adjust his daily work with it. On hearing this; the other person told him that if he agrees then let us try "Reiki". I had heard that for the first time, maybe I have read about it somewhere in the books but really did not know what the term meant.

He told us about himself and said that he is a certified Reiki master from Ludhiana. He told us that his life has changed completely after that one meeting with Anand Mai Maa. He was a bottler in city of Ludhiana and used to trade empty bottles with several factories for daily wages. He said that he is not literate and has tried his hands at many professions mainly the labor jobs. He has seen many ups and downs in his life but his life never got on track. Then one day by chance he happened to visit Anand Mai Maa's satsang (gathering). She wanted to demonstrate something with the help of one volunteer amongst the crowd. As he was also sitting there amongst the crowd and it so happened that she pointed towards him and instructed him to come up on the stage. He went up the stage and this was the turning point in his life. After that somebody amongst the crowd suggested him to apply for a Reiki seminar. Things started to change after that meeting. He applied for the seminar and finally got a call to attend one. He told us that it is rare to get selected for the seminar. Even after applying not all people get the chance to pursue it further. The ability to use Reiki is not taught in the usual sense, but is transferred to the student during a Reiki seminar/class. This ability is passed on during an attunement given by a Reiki master and allows the student to tap into an unlimited supply of life force energy to improve one's/other's health and enhance the quality of life. He went through one such seminar and it is after this he became a certified practitioner of Reiki. Soon the word began to spread about him and people started calling him for the Reiki sessions. As he told there was a time when people use to send personal vehicles to pick him up. He has done many reiki sessions till now. He told us that once a lady was feeling very low as her stomach was upset for many days. She became very thin as she could not eat anything for days. He then did reiki on her roti (Indian bread) and gave her the food. She began to digest the food after that and regained her health gradually. He shared many other incidents of reiki healing with us. When I asked him more about the process, he told me that it is the way of channelizing universal energy. But not everyone can do it, only the channels (human beings) can do so. He told us about the story of the saint from Japan, Mikao Usui, who got the reiki technique for the first time on mount kurama. He told us that there are lot of written material available on internet. We should consult that for full technique details. He just knows that he is a channel and can help others through this technique. He also shared several incidents where he has given Reiki to persons who have met with accidents by the roadside anonymously. Compassion for all beings is the key, he told us. I was at the receiving end of this conversation. At the end of it he asked us if we are interested in a live session of Reiki.

We said how is it possible?

He asked the commandant if he would like to have the same for his back pain. He ensured that his long aching back pain would be healed forever. Commandant immediately agreed for this. I was a silent watcher for the whole exercise. He asked commandant to lie upside down on his bed. He then took out his crystal bead bracelet from his bag and wore that in his right hand. He then came near to commandant and waved his hands all over commandants body as if he is cleaning something. He made sure that his hands do not touch his body. It appeared to me as some kind of a magical activity. But I could only observe it as he was still in that process. After doing this exercise for some time he stood at a distance from his body. He then recited a prayer in a low voice and stood facing commandant with his right palm facing towards the lower part of his spine. He stood in that position for some time and then asked commandant to try walking. As commandant put his foot down on the ground and as he walked he had a glitter in his eyes. He was amazed and said "where has the pain gone". Reiki master smiled at him. Commandant said it is a miracle as the pain which was unbearable for past nine years has finally gone. He said that "What not he has done to get relief from that pain but nothing worked" and now it has just vaporized. He felt a sense of gratitude for him. I was only an observer to this act. Then they both sat comfortably on their cots and the master told me about the whole process. I asked him about the purpose of wearing that crystal bracelet in his right hand. He told us that, he wore it for protection from negativities from other person's aura. The hand movement that he did was Aura cleansing. He said that we need to cleanse the aura before starting the Reiki session. It is for this activity that crystal bracelet is useful. After aura cleansing he uttered a prayer to his master for allowing him to become the channel for universal energy. He then redirected the universal energy towards commandant's base of the spine chakra. He always directs the energy on the closest chakra from the pain's location. After that the actual healing started. This was the whole process. He was nearly illiterate person as far as contemporary education is concerned but has become a good channel of universal energy. After seeing this I felt that education is necessary but still there are things that defy education. Now here is person in front of me who could heal another person but was not aware of the technicalities of the science. All three of us chatted for some more time and then I departed to my room. We need to attend the final discourse next morning before officially finishing the course.

Be Happy
Bhavatu Sabba Mangalam

A MEETING WITH
YOGI VISHWATMA

Winters in north India are quite cold and chilling. It was one of those winters in 2007 and I was in Dehradun Vipassana meditation centre (in state of Uttaranchal). The centre is built at front sloping side of one of the hills. City of Mussourie situated on another hill can be clearly seen from this centre. I reached Dehradun by bus and rented a shared auto rickshaw[38] to reach Mr Gupta's shop near Hotel Gaurab. Mr Gupta's address was mentioned in the Vipassana meditation monthly newsletter as a primary contact for the meditators. My family had enrolled for monthly newsletter. Mr Gupta had a wood work/carpenter shop and all the meditators are supposed to gather at his shop as the first meeting point. I reached there at about 2 pm. The shop was little inside a narrow lane besides Hotel Gaurab towards the left of the main road. I reached there and found couple of other meditators from different countries already waiting at the shop. I also settled and met Mr. Gupta. He said he will arrange for a private vehicle at around 2:30 pm. I kept my rucksack bag at the shop and came outside where I could see some meditators talking to each other. I introduced myself and we got engaged in a casual chat for some time. There I met one lady from Portugal. She use to generally visit India each year specifically the state of Goa for buying Handicrafts stuff, which later she use to trade in her own country. She said that she made it a point that she will attend one Vipassana meditation course each time she will be in India. We waited for another half an hour till that time some more meditators came for the course. Mr. Gupta use to arrange private vehicles for trip till the actual meditation centre. A previous group of meditators had already left at around 1 pm. He arranged for a private shared Jeep for our batch which arrived at around 2:30 pm. We were 7-8 meditators till that time and were ready to commute. Jeep owner charged Rs 25 from each person.

Jeep passed through city cantonment area and reached at Jantanwala village stop. It was the last bus stop on that route. The stop was adjacent to

---

[38] **Auto rickshaws** are a common means of public transportation in many countries in the world

the main road. All the private buses use to go till that stop. We all got out of the jeep and walked down the main road. We could easily see Dehradun Vipassana centre board on the bottom side of the front hill. Dehradun is a hilly terrain. There was one last hurdle to reach at the centre gates.

It was a shallow river stream. In winters the water level is so shallow that it can be crossed walking through it. The stream is full of white marble stones ranging from big ones to small ones. The water splashing through the stones looks very picturesque and refreshing. Only precaution one has to take is of the green algae and moss on some of the big stones which acts as a slippery surface. After crossing the stream barefoot with shoes in our hands we moved up the hill slope towards the centre gate. Everybody could see the big centre gates welcoming us with centre name written on it as "Dhamma Salila". The centre entry path was a little steep cemented slope. As we walked up slope and reached inside the centre premises, we asked for the registration office. A sevak directed us towards our right side. We entered the corridor leading us to the registration hall. After registration process (filling personal and previous course details if any, depositing our valuables if any) we were allotted residential rooms for the next 10 days. Residential quarters were mostly double occupancy. I was also allotted one of the rooms. Starting from that evening for the coming 9 Days we have to follow noble silence(refer code of discipline at Dhamma website). The 10th day was "Metta Day" where after sharing our merits with others, the vow of silence will finally be over. We can exchange words with other mediators on 10th day.

After taking some rest at our allotted rooms, we reached the centre hall in evening time where we were briefed by the centre manager about the basic rules we need to follow and certain things we should be aware of while in the centre. As the centre was at hilly terrain so we need to be cautious about any insects, snakes etc. As per the guidelines, we should not kill them under any circumstances.

Centre manager gave us the briefing about the five precepts (refer code of discipline at Dhamma website). After that we sat in the meditation for some time before retiring to our rooms at about 8:30 pm. The vow of silence has now officially started.

Next day meditation session started at 4:30 am in the morning. I heard the bell sound in the morning and got awake. I looked at my watch. It was 4:10 am in the morning. I woke up and brushed my teeth and finished up the basic chores and got ready for the morning session. We reached the hall with our blankets and sat there till 6:30 am bell rang. Each meditation session ends with a bell ring. It was time for morning breakfast and everybody reached the dining hall. We finished the breakfast and rested in our quarters till 8 am. I use to take bath at around 7:30 am and get ready for the next group meditation session starting at 8 am. Group meditations were compulsory so everybody has to attend these meditation sessions conducted at the main hall. Group meditation session started at 8 am and ended at 9 am and we moved out of the meditation hall. It was a small break of about 10 minutes and then everybody has to again reach the meditation hall for the next session. In this session teacher use to call each and every mediator and inquired them if they are facing any problems or doubts in understanding the basics of technique. If they have any query then they were allowed to ask the teacher but in low voice. From 11 am till 12 was lunch time. At about 12 noon everyone retired to their rooms for taking some rest before the next session at 1pm. After taking some break the next group meditation session started at 2:30 till 3:30 pm. After taking a small 10 minutes break we again sat for meditation in 3:30 pm to 5pm session. This was not a mandatory group meditation session. Then 5pm to 6pm was a tea break and then again from 6pm to 7pm was a group meditation. After 7pm there was a 10 minutes break after which everyone had to come to main meditation hall for group video discourse. The discourse went for about 1:30 hours followed up by a small half an hour meditation session. Everybody retired to their room at about 9 pm. If somebody has any queries or clarification points regarding the technique then they were allowed to have a word with the course teacher after 9 pm.

Two/Three days have passed by following the same time routine. In the morning time after 6:30 many mediators use to take nature's walk just beside the hill alongside pagoda. It was probably when I saw him for the first time. He was just walking out from the dining area towards the residential quarters. He was totally bald and had a drowsy face. Yet he was very erect and had a vigor and energy which could even beat the best of the child energy. He appeared to be very athletic and use to walk like as if he was running, never short of the energy even at such an old age. I guessed his age around 60. He used to wear a maroon robe and used to sit on high wooden chair like structure during the meditation sessions. He used to sit at the back in the last row on that four legged wooden platform. The course was going smoothly I was also concentrating on the usual meditation technique. I still remember that it was first time in that course, that a question was constantly hovering and continuously bugging my mind: "What is Nirvana?" - Can we at least understand that logically? What could have been the main blocks or clauses of it? I was into meditation as per the course timings but still this was the question that kept my mind occupied. I did not know what to do with this question. Based on my experiences of previous courses and my knowledge till that time I was gradually able to assimilate the same. It all happened during that course. I was able to grasp the fact that once all the senses are gone (die for sometime) then only it will happen. It's a "Dumb person's Jaggery. He won't be able to tell the taste". If somebody is telling the taste that means he has not seen that (note: I am using "seen" but I do not know what word should be used for that). The state or experience which is beyond the six senses cannot be explained by any of the six senses. Also one thing that I understood during the Vipassana discourses and based on other written material was that as we progress on path the births involve less senses for e.g. humans have 6 senses, next level birth (devlok) would also include 6 senses, next (Roop Bhrahmlok) would also have 6 senses and the next (Aroop Brahmlok) would only contain 1 sense i.e. of mind (other 5 senses are absent). So the next logical step would be that this mind sense would also die and that is nirvana. So atleast I could grasp that logically. This was one thought that converged after years of knowledge or who knows may be after many births. So it was clear that the person who experienced (actually experience is always used for the events perceived through 6 senses) nirvana for some time (as explained in the first stage called Sotappana, a stream enterer) will see his senses die for some time, all the 5 senses and finally the 6th one. This appeared logical to me but it was my own conclusion. On 6th day when I was meditating during the evening 6pm to 7 pm group sitting I was able to concentrate and I felt a state of Samadhi till 7 pm. As there was a break for about 10 minutes before the video discourse (by S.N Goenka played on a TV-Television) started. I did not leave my seat and I was in a state of Samadhi. The discourse started after people returned back from the break and I was still sitting at my seat in state of Samadhi. It continued till 8:15 pm. At the peak of it I could sense that Guruji's voice that was touching my ears started to die out. It started to fluctuate. At one time I was able to hear it but at next moment it was gone and I could even observe the dying out of the voice at my ear sense doors. I could make out that perhaps my ear sense is dying out. I continued in that Samadhi and then suddenly my body got tilted to 45 degrees above from the front but I was still sitting into the lotus posture. I was observing that state but then lady sevak saw my state of Samadhi and immediately went to the course teacher who was sitting next to TV and was not able to see me directly. He immediately stood up and moved towards me and tried snapping one finger at my ear. I opened the eyes immediately but then I closed them again slowly. He thought I was enjoying that state in which case sensory vibration might get multiplied. So as a next step he gave a little push to my pillow on which

I was sitting and I again opened my eyes and told him in low voice that I am observing it only and then again I closed my eye lids a little slowly. At this he might have thought that I was enjoying it. So he gave a strong vibratory push to my pillow and the next moment I was not in the lotus posture. I was out of that Samadhi state. Then I thought my sense of hearing was dying out slowly and could infer that similarly others will also die out. So eventually when all will die out for some time then only stream enterer, sotapanna (a brief nirvana state) will happen. That was an intense Samadhi experience. At first I thought that though I was ready to pass through that Samadhi experience, observing the sensations but still it got disrupted. I was still sitting at my allotted seat and thinking about the whole act just then a question came to my mind that "Why nature has pulled me out of this state?" An answer also came along that may be I have some more worldly desires through which I still need to pass, which I also knew that I have many such. So I left it to nature and remained equanimous with the thought that "Whatever happens, Happens for good". I still remember that I looked back towards him at the back row after that incident. He was also looking towards me as if watching the whole act curiously.

Everybody was allotted the cells (a small room for a meditator) in pagoda[39] on 7th day morning. Usually on 7th day meditators are allotted cells in pagoda. So I continued with my regular meditation practice at my allotted cell. The same regular routine continued for another two days. Then on 10th day the "Metta meditation" was given and after that our vow of silence was over. We could talk to each other now outside the main meditation hall. I saw meditators moving out walking on the cemented pathway from the main meditation hall talking to each other. I was moving silently to my residential room. I still remember I halted for some time in front of the hall. It is when I saw him approaching towards me. He was straight old face and walking like an erect stick in his maroon robe. He halted near me and we exchanged words. I asked him his age he replied it is 79 now. After talking a while, he cautioned me about my state which he witnessed from the back on the 6th day. He said that "He has also experienced such Samadhi state approximately a year back and advised me to keep an eye on the same. You should not enjoy the state and should always observe it". These were some of his guidance to me. I told

---

[39] A **pagoda** is a tiered tower with multiple eaves, built in traditions originating in historic East Asia or with respect to those traditions, common to Nepal, India, China, Japan, Korea, Vietnam, Burma and other parts of Asia. Refer Great Shwedagon pagoda located in Yangon, Myanmar.

him about all my thought process and my understanding of the nirvana. He then told me that he wanted to share one piece of information with me. He told me that same year in the month of July one fine day in the morning, he sat for his normal morning meditation and slowly he observed that his senses died one after another. And then he could not say anything about that state. I was amazed at the coincidence that the question I was having all through that course was now answered as a chance meeting with a Sotappana (a stream enterer). I was standing in front of a stream enterer talking to him about his experiences. I realized that Mother Nature is so powerful that "If we have any question then we always have an answer and it comes naturally". I was in a state of gratitude towards Mother Nature and my understanding of its laws was more mature after that meeting.

He shared with me that he has attained some siddhis(supernatural powers) in his earlier days. He told me that he had tried many techniques and meditations before getting Vipassana meditation. He told me that he meditated in Rishikesh (a place in Uttaranchal) jungles for about 14 years. He has also spent his time at many ashrams in Haridwar. He shared with me that after those intense meditation sessions in Rishikesh jungles, he attained "Gayatri Mantra siddhis" which many people are using for their personal benefits like business success etc. He warned me that all these powers are the field of earth domain only. For going deeper you need to leave these and move ahead in meditation. He said that he is contented after getting this technique in 2004. During our discussion, he said that spirituality is also a kind computer science which works with exact precision. Only thing here is that the computer (nature) has exact laws but they are little different from contemporary science laws. He said that he now lives in some ashram in Gujarat where he had one separate room and people there serve him food while he continues with his meditation. He also shared with me the signs of Kundalini awakening. After that we moved into his room and chatted for some time. I explained to him about my Samadhi experience and asked him again about nirvana and he replied that when all the senses are gone and he again stopped saying anything further. He could not say a word after that and looked towards the wall. Perhaps he was not able to express that through words. I asked him about his sleep patterns, he replied that he is now having only 2 to 2.5 hours of sleep and during that also he is always aware of the sensations. Another meditator also came in between and sat there for some time and then left his room without even saying a word. I continued talking to him. We talked about several ancient scenarios. He told me that Sanjay in Mahabharata had special sight through which he could see the battle field.

There I could get a first hand sense that these ancient stories could be real science. He also told me that there is one person in Jhansi who takes care of his travel expenses (railway tickets etc). He is a wandering soul now and roams around different places. He said that he once helped him with one of the Gayatri mantra siddhi's in his one personal job problem. He also gave him some fruit after which he was blessed with twin baby boys. At last just before leaving he handed me a five mukhi rudraksha and said that you should keep that in your pocket while going to your office. It will protect you from negativities. I did not know what was happening but I accepted that. After this I departed to my room. Next day in the morning just after the final discourse, I saw yogi Vishwatma walking out of the ashram premises in a sense of hurry to catch the train. I even could not bid him good bye. I looked at him one last time. As I was moving towards my room to pick up my luggage I saw our meditation course teacher and asked him to spare some time to discuss about that Samadhi state. He said that you should have come earlier. It is late now. He also left the ashram in a hurry. So this was my account of meeting with a stream enterer. He told me about his place in Gujarat where he occasionally stays and meditates. But I forgot that name. I sometimes long to meet him again but not sure whether I will get another chance some day. As per his advice I kept that Rudraksha[40] in my pocket for few days. After that I kept it somewhere in my house and forgot about it. It is recently that I have found it again in one of my drawer closets.

Life is turning now.. Waiting to see life's next move…

Yours Truly,
A Meditator,
Bhavatu Sabba Mangalam

---

[40] **Rudraksha**, also **rudraksh**, Sanskrit: *rudrākṣa* ("Rudra's eyes"), is a seed is traditionally used for prayer beads in hinduism.

A Water Yogi

It was the year 2007 and I was in Vipassana meditation center "Dhamma Salila" at Dehradun for a 10 day meditation course. We began the course with registration at the centre hall. We were allotted the residence quarters with double occupancy. We settled in our quarter and started the course with vow of silence for 9 days. We continued with the meditation as prescribed in the daily schedule starting from 4:30 am in the morning till 9 pm.

Daily Schedule:

4:00 am	Morning wake-up bell
4:30-6:30 am	Meditate in the hall or in your room
6:30-8:00 am	Breakfast break
8:00-9:00 am	Group meditation in the hall
9:00-11:00 am	Meditate in the hall or in your room according to the teacher's instructions
11:00-12:00 noon	Lunch break
12noon-1:00 pm	Rest and interviews with the teacher
1:00-2:30 pm	Meditate in the hall or in your room
2:30-3:30 pm	Group meditation in the hall
3:30-5:00 pm	Meditate in the hall or in your own room according to the teacher's instructions
5:00-6:00 pm	Tea break
6:00-7:00 pm	Group meditation in the hall
7:00-8:15 pm	Teacher's Discourse in the hall
8:15-9:00 pm	Group meditation in the hall
9:00-9:30 pm	Question time in the hall
9:30 pm	Retire to your own room--Lights out

On the 10th day the maître sadhana (Metta meditation) was given; after which vow of silence was officially over at around 10 am. Though the mediators can now talk to each other and exchange their views freely while they still have to be in centre premises. Also meditators still needs to follow silence inside the main meditation hall. The course was officially completed next morning after a final video discourse by Guruji Shri S.N Goenka during the morning session from 4:30 am to 6:30 am.

The 10th day is very important as after the vow of silence is over we get to know about other meditators, their views and stories. We meet people from all walks of life and across different economic and cultural backgrounds. I met a person from Italy who used to be a tourist guide there and after some personal family mishaps he is now full into meditation. I met a professor from University of Sydney. I met many ascetics from Haridwar, scientist / intellectuals from across the world. The free thought exchange, meeting with people from different backgrounds was really an environment fostering personal growth. It is on the 10th day of this course that I met that yogi from Shankracharya hermitage. He was very soft spoken person with beard and moustache on his face as if he has not shaved it even once. He was about 5 feet 5 inches with a dusky complexion and was wearing a yellow dhoti[41] and a robe on the upper part. He was residing in the adjacent room where he was talking to another person after the lunch time (lunch is served at 11 am and next meditation session starts at 1pm). Most of us after finishing the lunch were engaged in casual interactions with each other till 1 pm. Other person was a retired Border Security Force commandant[42] and they both were engrossed in some conversation when I entered the room. We greeted each other and exchanged the information about each other's place and profession. I also sat there and we talked for quite some time. This was the beginning of the conversation and it continued till 1pm when we departed for meditation session. The conversation continued again during the non group meditation hours. The evening discourse started at 7:15 pm till 8:30 pm and everybody left for their residence quarters for the last time. We three met again at his quarter and discussed again about our views and continued our discussions. First the retired commandant told his story of mantra given to him by a swami. He told us that when he was very young probably 6-7 years, he was once left alone in his juice shop. His father had some personal work, so he left the juice corner for some time. His shop was at main market in the city of Dehradun, India. He was supposed to look after the shop for some time. He said, during that time a swami came at his shop. He said that "he was

---

[41]   The **_dhoti_**, also known as veshti, mundu, pancha or mardani, is a traditional men's garment worn in the Indian subcontinent.

[42]   **_Commandant_** is a title often given to the officer in charge of a military (or other uniformed service) training establishment or academy.

feeling very thirsty". "I offered him the sweet lime juice", commandant said. Swami said that he didn't have any money. I said that I do not want money and requested him to please quench his thirst by drinking the sweet lime. He took it finally and felt quenched after drinking the juice. He smiled towards me and after that he came closer to me and uttered few words in my ear. He said that this is mantra for body healing. Do not misuse it and do not out show this to others. He said that whenever you face any injury then you should recite this mantra and your wound will heal instantaneously. This sounded a little magical to me at that time. After that Commandant got a call on his mobile phone and left the room saying "excuse me". I wanted to know what happened to his mantra story but after he left I was alone with yogi. It is now that yogi started sharing his personal experiences. He told me that he left his home at the age of 16. He now lives in Shankracharya hermitage. He told me that he had one elder brother who was engineering topper and use to love mathematics. He is now working with British secret services and solves complex mathematical problems. He lives in U.K. Then he told me about himself that after leaving home he went to Shankracharya hermitage and studied there. He said that they use to go for daily alms begging as bhikkus[43]. We discussed about several topics one of them being "How the soul enters the earth environment" and how it is transferred to the grazing animal like cow when cow eats the grass and finally comes in the cow's milk and then ultimately to the mother's womb. I did not have any veracity of this statement. After touching several such points during our discussion he then told me a very specific story that there are infinite sciences hidden in nature and during one such yugas[44] cycle only a few of them comes out. Then he narrated one such experience from his life. He said many years back he once left the hermitage for outer worldly living. At that time, he also did not knew for how many days. He wandered for many days and nights before settling in one of the nearby villages. One night he felt motivated to stare at a small point on his room wall. He tried this activity for very long hours (about 15-16 hours) without even blinking his eyes. As he was narrating, I was feeling "How could anybody do this and that too without even blinking his eyes". He clarified that in fact he did blink his eyes but for most of the time he stared it straight looking at that point. After about 15 hours his eyes got strained and he felt drowsy and was about to sleep when something strange happened. He

---

[43] A **bhikkhu** (Pāli) is an ordained Buddhist monk.
[44] **Yuga** in Hindu philosophy is the name of an epoch or era within a four age cycle.

saw that the same point has now been converted into water. He saw that the instead of the wall he now saw water on the whole wall and could not grasp that event. He thought that his mind is perhaps playing games with him. He felt really tired and slept for long after this incident. In the days to come after that incident he saw a strange thing happening to him. He could now see the water level of the area land. For few days he could not understand what is happening to him but it continued to happen. Then word got out through word of mouth publicity, that there is yogi who could see water level under the ground. Then he started to get request from village people to come to their village and help them in locating the underground water for new up-coming wells. Wherever he sees the water level is high he would tell the villagers and they could verify that by digging the well. His hit ratio was cent per cent. People started to call him water yogi. He now started getting invitation from different villages across that region. They also started to offer him money and gifts for his services. They would even send their personal vehicles to bring him to the proposed well digging sites. He has now become a local celebrity in his own way. They use to give him money, clothes, sweets etc. His ego got inflated and flattered after these incidents and he also started to feel celebrity status. He even started to charge good price for such visits. And as his ego trend took a sharp upward rise suddenly one day he observed that he could not see the underground water level anymore. He did not know what to do with the villager's requests. He could not say no the ones who came to him for water level verification. He slowly started to lose it as the water levels suggested by him were verified negatively. People now started to figure out that he is making fake claims about the water level. He told that he randomly suggested them the well digging site as he could not see it anymore. Soon people began to notice this and stopped calling him. Some even abused him for making false claims and soon the celebrity phase was over. One day he ran away from there; introspected and came to conclusion that perhaps he started to misuse the gift given to him by nature for his personal benefits. He again went to the Shankracharya hermitage after this incident and again started to serve and continued with their daily alms begging.

He said finally that there are infinite sciences hidden in nature and if one focuses on anything, something will be revealed. We need to serve others with the same. Serving others is the biggest purpose of our lives here.

Be Happy
Bhavatu Sabba Mangalam

SATURN RINGS – A NIGHT WITH ASTRONOMERS

❖

It was a normal day and I was doing some basic research for building observatory for night sky gazing. I was also interested in buying a telescope for my personal use and came across few links and videos regarding the same on the internet. I tried few options for buying it online. Though I did not have any previous experience in astronomy apart from high school memories but still for quite some time I was feeling that I should have my own telescope. The thought of seeing the night sky, the moon and the planets through a telescope was mesmerizing and giving me enough thrill to continue exploring the same. It was during this search that I found a website link on internet for an organization named "KhagolVishwa" (www.kvindia.org) where I found advertisement for an upcoming star gazing program on their website to be held in May 2013. It immediately caught my attention and I called up the contact numbers given on the website. I called up Mayuresh the main coordinator/organizer of the event. He was also a founder of this organization for amateur astronomers. I asked about the fees and the way it would be organized as it was written in advertisement that it will be conducted overnight. He told me the details of the program fees and the way of conducting workshop. He told me that we need to take a public bus/personal vehicle till the program site. In case of those who prefer public transport all the amateurs/astronomers will gather at Swargate bus station. Last bus will leave by 7:30 pm. All persons have to arrange their own dinner. It will not be served at the site.

As per his instructions I left for bus station on Friday evening and parked my motor bike at a common point (Swargate Vipassana meditation centre). I reached the bus station and inquired inside for the exact stop from where Panshet(star gazing site location) bus will leave. As I reached at the stop I asked a boy standing there with a group,

"When would last bus to Panshet leave?"

He replied that "They are also waiting for the bus".

I asked them "Are they going for the night sky gazing program"? They said yes.

119

There was a couple coordinating with all the participants present there. They were instructing all the participants going for the program. Gathering mostly had teenage boys and girls. Apart from this, some families (husband wife and their kids mostly around 10-12 years) were also present. Everybody was eagerly waiting for the bus. Bus was little late. In the meantime I took some snacks and a cold drink at the station. Bus came by and everybody boarded in a hurry as it was a public stand. Bus got occupied completely by the program participants. There was hardly any seat left for any other public passengers. It was already night time (dark) outside. Soon the bus with all the passengers speeded up towards the actual star gazing site i.e. Panshet. We reached Panshet bus stop the last one on that route by around 8:30 pm. Everyone came out and gathered there for a small briefing by coordinators. They guided us towards the site. Everyone followed the coordinators after leaving the bus stop. They have arranged for few torch lights as it was a jungle area and we had to walk till the actual event site. We followed the torch lights and reached at a primary school amidst hills on three sides. It was getting little cold at the night time and the organizers announced that we can proceed with our dinner there on the ground floor. After that we will move on the top floor starting further activities. I did not bring any Tiffin with me as I was alone those days. My family had gone to my home town. I had some snacks with me and everybody started to have their dinner. There was one prominent group of youngsters probably from one college. They all gathered in a circle and exchanged their food items. It was a nice get together at night time under the moon. Very rarely we get such a chance of having dinner under stars amidst the hills. Many participants were still reaching at the site in their personal vehicles. It was basically a group activity at night. After a while organizers announced the night itinerary of the event. I also listened to it with attention. Everybody was requested to move at top of the school building. As we reached at top of the building we could see that Khagol Vishwa had arranged for a projector and a screen. Chairman asked us to occupy the floor as per our convenience. It was a different feeling for me just sitting under the open night sky with stars all around. With a limited visibility at night, I could easily imagine beauty of the site during day time. It seems there was not any other building around. We occupied the seats on the floor. I had brought a bedsheet with me in case it was needed. I just sat on that besides three other boys. They were from a software company in Pune, India and had active interest in astronomy. We chatted and shared our views till the time projector was setup. After about 15-20 minutes the chairman called for our attention and told us that we will first be starting with a presentation about the group, its formation and growth. After that we will settle for night sky gazing program. After a while presentation started and he told us about the formation and growth of organization in past eight years. He was the first one to start it. Then people came along and group expanded. They have a good mix of students and amateurs. Many of us asked them few question about the funding and collaborative projects with ISRO (Indian Space Research Organisation). He answered them humbly and told us briefly about such projects.

I really enjoyed the presentation and then he introduced us to the relevant persons who will be responsible for conducting the night sky gazing session. I was waiting for this one. They announced to form two groups amongst us.

Both the groups occupied different areas of the roof top floor. Everybody was asked to lie down at the floor in circles. There are two circles now. Each of the group instructors was standing in the middle with a sharp laser light in his hand and everyone else was lying on the floor in circular fashion so that everyone could see the person in centre with their foot towards the centre of the circle. Once everybody got settled, he started explaining the night sky. He explained us about the popular constellation like Saptrishi and ursa major / minor etc. He was showing these with the help of laser light. I felt as if I was really pepping into the ocean of stars now. This was my first experience of one on one meeting with stars and constellation. The laser lights are visible like light rods used in star war movies and many a times the two lasers use to intersect each other. My imagination was flowing wild as if some kind of sky war is going on. This was extensive session and they showed us some of the constellations and were answering our queries. As everybody was focusing on the stars in the major constellation, we saw a moving star. The instructor told us that if we look carefully at the star then we will find that it is not blinking. Yes, he was right; star was a non-blinking one, we concluded immediately. I looked again and thought that it is not following the basic condition of a star. A star always blinks. The guide told us that it is actually a satellite revolving around earth. This was the first time I saw a satellite in the sky. It was such a simple discovery yet so important one. It once again proved to me that theory and practical should go hand in hand for proper understanding. I could see some children in this group. This would definitely be a good satellite demonstration session for them. After continuing for some more time the session ended. The chairman announced that we will have a small tea break at penultimate floor. Everyone got up and moved down the stairs towards the penultimate floor. As we entered the room I saw a lady was preparing tea for us. It was around 2 am in the morning. It was night time and there was no staff member there. She was from one of the organizer's family. This showed me the gratitude and dedication inside the organization. The chairman was a simple but visionary person. He had a vision for the organization and his family was fully supporting him in his work. He also brought his two kids to participate in this workshop. So in a way he was no different than us. Everybody enjoyed the tea at such a late hour with some biscuits. It was really a treat for me in the coolness of that night.

After finishing up the tea we went on the top floor again and now the chairman announced that we will be observing the Saturn planetary rings through a telescope. This was the star attraction of the program. This would again be a first time experience for me. They took some more time to setup the telescopes. After they finished the setup, everybody queued up at the telescope. Slowly but smoothly I was moving towards the Saturn. There were two telescopes to balance the load. I was little excited to see the rings. And then finally the turn came. As I pepped into the lens, I was mesmerized at the sight of beautiful rings. "Amazing" I said! They were not that big as I have imagined or have seen on many television channels. Yes they were good. Probably some day I will see them through high resolution telescope. Just before me was a small kid waiting for his turn. He saw the rings and then I had a brief discussion with his family. His father used to work in a private bank. They had brought the kid for workshop due to his huge fascination for the night sky. The kid was really enthusiastic one. I chatted with his father who also had a taste for astronomy. During the free flow discussion he told me about a person who has built a mobile planetarium. That person now arranges for paid visits in city schools. Sometime he also visits village schools for the show. They were charging Rs 50 for each kid. I thought it was a nice model as many kids who could not come to city planetarium would get to see the planets and related information at their doorsteps. In a way he was selling "astronomy" dreams. This was a good business model perhaps, I thought. He will be able to recover his fixed investment in some years. Some more business ideas passed my mind while he was narrating this story.

After this session they showed us one more presentation. It was one of their ambitious projects related to monsoon tracking which they executed few months back. They told us that they got a chance to collaborate with meteorological department on that project. Khagol Vishwa named it project "Meghdoot". I found it little unusual. They went to kanyakumari (last point, south of India) and started tracking the clouds (aka monsoon) as they moved along the coast and inside. They showed us the project snaps in which they were travelling in their vehicle tracking the clouds. This was a little unusual site for me. I could not believe that these types of project could actually be executed. I could hardly imagine about them but yet here it was. Then they showed us some slides about a big crater in Lonar around Maharashtra. The crater is assumed to be formed around 50,000 years back by a meteor hit. It was a huge crater and now encompasses varied flora and fauna. It was a chief research site for city universities and flora and fauna enthusiasts. I felt good at knowing that such sites do exist nearby my place i.e. Pune. They told us they are actively working on towards declaring this site as world heritage site by United Nations. They are working for this cause for quite some time and hopeful that one day it will be a World heritage site. It was almost morning time till the workshop got finished. I had some personal discussion with the chairman who was also a journalist in one of the leading Maharashtra newspaper named Maharashtra Times. I asked him regarding the funding for these projects. He told us that he had some projects for which talks are going on for the possibility of collaboration with ISRO. He informed me that all the students/participants are bearing the costs themselves.As the discussion grew further, I shared my interest of building up an indigenous observatory for kids. He shared quite a lot of information regarding the same. He gave me a contact for one person who was involved in building observatory for government projects. That person has an independent company for Observatory building and works in many Asian countries on project basis. I thanked him for such a nice workshop and wished him all the luck for doing such a nice work. Workshops like these can have far reaching effect on young science baton holders. He was truly a light for young ones. I felt that activities like this should be promoted and should flourish as they also give us some time to think and give a chance to see our own beloved universe closely.

I felt like sharing few lines in gratitude:

> Stars Stars are many in sky,
> Moon Moon is one jewel in sky,
> Night sky is the one to see,
> Night sky is the one for me,
> Mr. Saturn is one and the same,
> With lovely rings for my eyes,
> Kids charging, Kids bubbling
> For "Saturn Rings" to see their eyes.
>> In gratitude to Khagol Vishwa (www.kvindia.org)

After a long discussion; very rich and fulfilling night came to an end. The day broke and I could now see the beauty of that site surrounded by hills. We left for bus stop. As we all reached at the local bus stop we cheered and took a final snap. The memories are still with me and for days to come…

For me in one line: "It was a romantic date with Saturn rings"

I still remember that night sometimes.

Be Happy
Bhavatu Sabba Mangalam

Travel To Mars And Jupiter

◆━◆━◆

ASTRAL TRAVEL TO THE MARS

(This article was written for a magazine 'Life Beyond', published by the Life Beyond Foundation, Harnik House, 9 Sadhu Vaswani Road, Pune, 411001)

"Life Beyond" does not necessarily mean life after death. Life beyond means existence of a life beyond the physical **plane**. Such a life beyond the physical plane does exist. This is proved by one of my experiments, in the Yoga Shastra. This experiment is of Astral Travel. I am a student of 'ADHYATMA' AND 'YOGA'. For last 24 years I am practicing this subtle science, therefore I could do this experiment. I had read and heard of many miracles done by Yogis. But as I am a scientist I was not ready to believe these miracles, unless they are proved by scientific methods. I met many masters in this field but nobody was ready to do any scientific experiment. So I thought of studying this science myself, to take self experience. I got many experiences but here I will restrict to only one - an Astral Travel to the Mars. In the year 1975 during the month of July, I read in newspaper that America is going to launch a spaceship to land on Mars, a Planet 340 millions of miles away from our Earth. Up till that date there was no definite information about the Mars.

After reading this news I thought of doing an experiment of getting the knowledge of the Mars by the ways of "ADHYATMA". If I can succeed in getting a definite knowledge, 'Adhyatma' can be called as a definite science. There was a chance to test this knowledge by comparing the reports of the American spaceship Viking-1. This test was very important and so my scientific mind took this challenge.

One day, late in July 1975, I went into 'DHYANA' (meditation) and then into 'SAMADHI' to get knowledge about the Mars. In this Samadhi I felt that I was standing on the Mars. But when I came out from Samadhi to the physical level I forgot everything. Only the impression of going to the Mars remained. Being a scientist I was not happy with this experiment, so I discarded this attempt.

On August 10, 1975 at 9.15 am I again went into Samadhi, when I left my body, I left this earth and went straight to the Mars. At this time I had **no feeling of**, and had no relations with, my physical body, my home and this earth. I felt that I was physically standing on the Mars. I did not feel that I travelled from the Earth to the Mars because this projection of Astral Body was instantaneous. The moment I left my body on the Earth, I was on the Mars, 340 millions of miles away.

I felt that I was standing on one open ground. There was red coloured soil on that ground, just like that we see in Konkan area of India. I could see up to the Horizon - all was red coloured. I wondered to see that there was no tree, no plant and no grass. I saw here and there but I could not see any human being or any other animal. Astonished, I saw in the sky if birds were present, but I could not see a single bird in the sky.

While looking at the sky I saw the sky quite colorful, just like the evening sky on the Earth. I saw blue sky with red, yellow and green colours. It was pleasant to look at that colourful sky of the Martian evening. After observing the sky of the evening of the Mars I turned my eyes to the ground again. On my left hand side I saw a dried-up rivulet. Only the sand and rocks were present and they, too, were red in colour. There was no water at all. The rocks were red in colour, but I could see on those rocks, some black patches caused by old, dead and darkened moss.

Then I tried to look down at my feet. I could not see any insect on the ground. While observing this ground I came to know that I was not able to see my feet, though I felt that I was standing on my feet on the ground, I had feeling of having a head, eyes, ears and neck.

I could not hear any sound. I was looking here and there by turning my neck and head.

As I was looking, a breeze of wind came. I felt that breeze with my touch-sense. That breeze was cool. From that cooling touch I thought that there was moisture in the wind, because the coolness was just like that we feel in rainy seasons. Apart from cool touch of the wind everything there was barren and dry. I felt that heat was coming out of my body. If we run for an important work with tension on the mind, we feel such a sense of heat coming out from neck and face - exactly the same sense I felt while standing on the Mars.

After observing all these facts, suddenly, I returned to the Earth, in to my body. I came to consciousness. Then I saw the watch, it was 9.30 am. So I was in deep Dhyana and Samadhi for only 15 minutes. After coming to senses, immediately, I wrote whatever I could remember. I have put it before you.

This was the event of August 10, 1975 i.e. full 10 days before the launching of Viking 1, on August 20, 1975. Because I wanted to perform a scientific experiment I wanted this to publish but our newspapers paid no importance to this work and no paper published my report.

I prepared a circular and sent it to many institutions. I sent my report to the President and the Prime Minister of India; but got no response. So I published this data in two Marathi Magazines 'SANTAKRIPA' June issue, published on 21st May 1976 and 'DHARMIK', July issue published in June 1976. Following are the points published in the magazines:--

1: There is no life on the Mars- no human being, no animal, no bird, no insects, no trees, no plants, no life of any kind, no living creature of any kind.

2: There is no water on the Mars -neither flowing water like river, stream etc., nor stagnant water like lakes, ponds, seas, etc.

3: There is moisture i.e. water content in atmosphere as is evident from cool breeze of air.

4: Environment is dry and barren.

5: Sky is blue with evening colours like red, yellow, and green.

6: Formerly, in the long past, there were rivers on Mars as indicated by the empty riverbed.

7: There must have been life on the Mars in remote past as is indicated by presence of dried up and blackened Algae on the rock surfaces.

8: The soil, rocks, pebbles etc. were all red in colour like those in Konkan- Goa side.

9: The ground on Mars is just like that of the Earth containing mountains valleys, stones, pebbles etc. It does not resemble like that of the Moon, with craters.

10: The breeze, which I felt was cold, it indicated the presence of water content in air. On August 10, 1975, I saw all these twenty one points and sub points within 15 minutes' time, ten days prior to the launching of Viking - 1, which was launched on August 20, 1975. It took energy of thousands of scientists for many years, it took billions of dollars' financial energy, it used ample and dreaded atomic energy and it took full eleven months to reach the Mars, about 340 millions of miles away, and the reports sent by this Viking-I were the same as mine. So my energy equals to the sum of all the above energies.

I had given 21 points and sub points on August 10, 1975. Till that date it was held by all scientists that on the Mars the human beings have prepared canals of water for agriculture.

Even "Mariner 9" had given photographs of these canals in 1973. So I had to face all sorts of people calling me a great fool.

On 21st July 1976, the first report of Viking came on the earth. All newspapers published 'Possibility of life on Mars', in big titles. So many friends rushed to me saying 'You are wrong'. But I was so confident that I told them calmly to wait and watch. From 23rd July 1976 onwards reports came that there is no possibility of life on the Mars as there is no water at all. Red colour of the soil and rocks was confirmed. Sky and its colours were confirmed.

Even the water-content of air was confirmed. Photographs dispatched by Viking proved the colours and description of the ground that it has no craters, like Moon. Out of my 21 points 20 were proved to be correct. Only one point of presence of old, dead, dark moss was not confirmed. But its reason is that the Viking scraped only the soil and not the rocks. It is well known that the moss gathers on rocks and never grows in soil. As Viking did not scrape the rocks it did not give the report of moss. That does not mean that I was wrong. Thus my success is cent percent.

It is to be noted that much later in 1987 the Pathfinder reported the presence of water on the Mars, in the long past. Spirit and other spaceships confirm the same.

From this successful experiment the following points are established:

1: Spiritual science is a real and perfect science.
2: There is presence of some Astral Body, which can leave the physical body and go away. I had left my own body and had gone to the Mars. The "One" who had gone to the Mars had a body, a head, eyes, sense of touch etc. Thus sensory organs are present in this body. This body is called as 'Linga Deha' in Sanskrit. Taittiriya Upanishad calls it 'Vijnanamaya Kosha'.
3: The speed of this body is fantastic. I performed the travel in a Dhyana of 15 minutes only. Out of these 15 minutes going through Dhyana to Samadhi and coming out again, must have taken at least 12-15 minutes. So no time is spent in traveling 700 millions of miles. It is evident from American reports that the transmission of data from the Mars to the earth took 20 minutes, even though the transmission is effected with the velocity of light (187352.5 miles per second). The Astral Body seems to have a velocity 100 times faster than light. That is why, traveling was not felt by me.
4: As the presence of Linga Deha (Astral body) is proved and as it is also proved that the Linga Deha can leave the physical body and go

away, it is imperative to believe that at the time of Death this Linga Deha leaves the physical body and goes away.

5: As my Linga Deha could stay without the assistance of my physical body for some time, it is evident that it can stay without a physical body for any length of time. Same thing happens after the Death of physical body.

6: This experiment thus proves the presence of life beyond the physical level.

Second Astral Travel to the Mars:

After success in the first expedition, Marathi newspaper 'Tarun Bharat' published an article on it admitting full success. Then I got some challenges out of which I selected one. It challenged me to tell what will happen to Viking 1 and 2, because Viking 2 was nearing Mars. On 12th Aug.1976, I went into Samadhi at night at 10 pm and went to the Mars. I felt that I was standing on the Mars. The sky was dark. On that dark background, I saw two coppery red objects, moving from my right hand side to left. The one on left was smaller and round. Second was oblong. I understood from within that the left was Viking 1 and right Viking 2. As I saw, Viking 1 stopped and came in reverse to meet Viking 2. There was circular arrangement on tail end of Viking I and on front of Viking 2 for docking. Viking 1 touched the front of Viking 2. There was a rotation of about 45 degrees around the long axis.

Viking 1 turned from above downwards from my side, while Viking 2 rotated from below upwards from my side. A perfect docking was to happen but suddenly some thing happened and the experiment was postponed. Viking I detached and moved fast to my left. Bigger Viking 2 followed it slowly. Actually the experiment was gaining success, but the scientists suspected some mistake and ordered Viking 1 to detach and go away. My conclusion was that first the experiment will be postponed and then will be cancelled.

My report was published in 'Tarun Bharat' dated 22nd Aug.1976. I sent a copy to the Director of American Embassy. Mr. Bayes appreciated my spiritual work, but said on 18th August that I would be wrong because such an experiment was not fixed at all and there were no mechanisms for them to dock. However, on the 7th Sept. 1976 a NASA news was published that such an experiment will take place on the 12th Sept. 1976. The NASA news approved the direction, which I had told that the Vikings are moving from my right to left side, because NASA published that they were moving from the east to the west. We know that the east is plotted on the right side and west on the left. It proved that some of my bodies stood on the Mars, because scientists used the directions of the Mars and not of the earth. Later on the docking program was first postponed and then cancelled. It proved that I could peep into the future for at least one month. It was a grand success. Here also my Vijnanamaya Kosha had gone to the Mars.

On the 12th of Sept 1976, the docking did not take place. There was no news either.

Then I read news that the program is postponed. Then the news came that the program is cancelled. Everything happened as I had foreseen. It was a grand success of spiritual science.

I would like to tell one amusing experience. When my report about Viking 1 and 2 was published in the 'Tarun Bharat', two professors of physics approached me and said, "If any object is in motion in the space, according to physics, it will never stop and will never take reverse motion. From where can it take energy to create a reverse motion?" I told that I saw it happen, with my own eyes; how can it happen I do not know. The answer was given in the NASA report dated 7th Sept. 1976 that the Viking 1 is followed by Viking 2. Viking 1 will fire its anti-rocket and will cease its motion. Then it will fire another rocket to gain reverse motion. Then it will meet Viking 2 for docking and transfer of works.

What physics did not know and what the Director of the American embassy did not know was understood by my spiritual power, though I was sitting in my home in Pune. My experiment was published all over and one scientist from NASA team, namely Miss Vatsala came to see me in Pune. She discussed with me nicely with full interest and on my request she agreed to be a chairperson for the annual symposium of the Veda Vidnyana Mandal, in June 1978. I was satisfied to see that at least one scientist took interest in my work.

By Dr P V Vartak
Bhavatu Sabba Mangalam

Forgiveness Prayer

To Universe,

Today I am willing to forgive each and every
person that has come into my life.

Please take this message to all the souls/beings.

Be Happy,

Bhavatu Sabba Mangalam,

www.dhamma.org

Gratitude Exercise

(Write/Think the name of persons, things, situations you are grateful for in your life)

I am grateful for …

BE HAPPY

BHAVATU SABBA MANGALAM

www.dhamma.org

Printed in the United States
By Bookmasters